**"P'torra must not possess
secret of randomness,"
said Slenth.**

The reptile's talons clicked on the floor to emphasize his concern. "Must *never* learn of its nature."

Ralston struggled to find the words to tell his friend when a soft click alerted him. In the shadows at the far end of the hall he saw a darker figure. A glint of light caught the focusing muzzle of an energy weapon.

Without thinking, Ralston threw his arms around Slenth and drove forward. The two of them smashed hard into the wall just as a sizzling blue torrent of energy ripped through the space where Ralston had been. The Nex dropped to the floor and had his weapon in action before Ralston could recover his senses.

The computer console blinked slowly, numbers still solemnly marching across the screen. Whoever had put the spy devices in his office now alerted campus security about the firefight in progress. Would this save them—or doom them?

THE WEAPONS OF CHAOS

BOOK 3: COLORS OF CHAOS
ROBERT E. VARDEMAN

ACE BOOKS, NEW YORK

This book is an Ace original
edition, and has never been
previously published.

COLORS OF CHAOS

An Ace Book/published by arrangement with
the author

PRINTING HISTORY
Ace edition/June 1988

ISBN: 0-441-11384-2

Ace Books are published by The Berkley Publishing Group,
200 Madison Avenue, New York, New York 10016.
The name ''ACE'' and the ''A'' logo
are trademarks belonging to Charter Communications, Inc.
PRINTED IN THE UNITED STATES OF AMERICA

10 9 8 7 6 5 4 3 2 1

For Geo. and Lana,
good friends
on "the never-ending flight
of future days."

ONE

THE MAGNESIUM FLARES boiled away lakes of frozen ammonia and sent hot winds gusting through the forest of ragged lava spires. The spawn of Beq surged before the wavefront, screaming in agony as the intense heat ripped away life and thought from his vaporous body. It rose and twisted in midair riding the concussion, vainly seeking escape.

The last thought before it dissipated totally in temperatures exceeding those of melting water ice was of its spawn partner. Then came a burning followed by a darkness so total that it defied even the spawn of Beq's philosophy to define.

Deep within the sheltering bulk of the planet, the other product of Beq's fission-spawning coalesced into a tight ball and rolled with the shuddering impacts of the bombs on the planetary surface.

"Will it never end?" Beq's spawn moaned. It tightened even more and sank to the floor of the chamber. Warmth spread into its body and provided sustenance—and a small measure of courage. Pressed into the lava-fed warmth of the floor, it remembered nostalgically the moments before Beq's fission and the joy of that reproduction. When it had been fully Beq, the spawn had felt the need for renewed vigor, added mental capacity, new curiosity to fuel intellectual search.

The spawn of Beq reveled in that comforting memory. Knowing that its spawn-twin had been trapped on the surface when the enemy began bombardment filled it with a void that refused to yield to explanation. It was no longer the spawn of

1

Beq, it knew. Not with its fission-twin gone. It now assumed
the full name of Beq.

The burden of this sudden and unexpected solitude made
the gaseous body quiver and ripple with self-pity. Alone
again. It would require at least a hundred planetary revolutions around the distant, pale star before spawn time came
and allowed it to produce another partner. Life proved so
unfair.

"Damn this war!" Beq cried.

"We failed to detect their war vessels when they entered
our system," said another in the council chamber. The advi-
sors had gathered in this safe underground vault hewn from
solid obsidian for a routine meeting, only to be told of the
devastating raid within minutes of convening. "The mechanicians who allowed this outrage will be thrown into the plasma
torch!"

Beq composed itself, sending out feathery tendrils to brush
across the surface of feeding pillars. The warmth from the
planetary core fed it, giving the creature the energy necessary
for more complex thought. Beq sighed, gusting out a thin
current of ammonia that immediately cooled and turned to
crystalline splinters in the air. It preferred drifting on the
surface winds, scattering its body into a transparent veil, and
returning—almost—to the most primitive state possible. Only
in this animalistic condition did Beq get its most innovative
ideas.

"Our surface defenses have prevailed," said this day's
head of the ruling committee. The creature floated to the top
of the vaulted chamber and thickened its tendrils to gain the
others' attention. "Twelve enemy war vessels are no more.
Another ten have been driven off. The planet is again safe."

Beq pondered this. Safe? How was it possible that the
enemy penetrated planetary defenses so easily? Beq tried not
to think of its lost spawn-twin. The toll had been heavy,
indeed, because of laxness in detecting the attacking fleet
until the sizzling magnesium bombs superheated the surface
and brought death and destruction to any creature unfortunate
enough to be exposed. The ruling committee needed to prevent future tactical forays against their planet.

"Our mechanicians are at fault," Beq said, after considering the issue for a full planetary rotation. "They allowed the enemy to elude our far-flung observation web."

"Impossible," flared another creature. Its anger showed in the vibrant color of its tendrils circling a lava column. Reds and yellows glowed to an unhealthy level, then cooled to a more controlled green and blue. "I personally oversee the detection system. It functions perfectly. How dare Beq make such allegations without proof?"

"Proof?" asked Beq. Why did the others always insist on physical proof when mentation provided the answer to any question? Beq saw in them the failing of the race. Empirical concerns should never overwhelm the philosophical. Beq formulated its response carefully, knowing that no one else on the ruling committee took the joy it did on soaring on the high-velocity, upper atmospheric winds, defying death by dissipation, returning to a level where ideas boiled without the restrictions of civilized behavior. It was in such a state that Beq—or Beq before fissioning—first conceived of the chaos equations. And it was in such a carefree euphoric state that Beq solved those equations and allowed the lesser mentality mechanicians to build the ultimate weapon.

Those mechanicians to whom it revealed the weapon design had been careless in releasing the weapon, more a concept than a physical entity. Beq had fought long to gain the ruling committee's approval for the project, but it had prevailed when the enemy had countered every other weapon directed against both planetary stronghold and space-borne fleet. Beq had seen that the enemy—fixed form beings with eerily warm bodies—commanded vast resources from a hot world and cunningly avoided most attacks directed against them.

It had floated on ammonia winds until the notion of a chaotic weapon came to it. Beq had watched the chaos field being launched, a space-warping field that changed nature's laws in ways seemingly random but controlled by Beq's mathematics and the elaborate command center at its heart. That field would drift through space, intrude on the enemy home world, and create havoc unparalleled in the history of Beq's race. The enemy's sun going nova was the least of the disruption—but it would be the most emphatic.

Working its unfelt, unseen chaos, the device would visit upon the enemy's world unpredictable storms. Familiar chemical reactions would no longer proceed. And worse for the fixed form enemy, their biologic systems would begin to fail. The laws of heredity would be violated, producing sports and mutations of obscene proportions.

Beq's body elongated as it twisted into a figure-eight pattern around two warm rock posts. There might be more, Beq thought. Here it envied those empiricists who floated and observed rather than working through every conceivable outcome mathematically. Beq's unfamiliarity with solid body life forms prevented it from making a positive estimate of other effects induced by the chaos field. Beq's surface rippled as it considered the possibility of its weapon disrupting thought processes by changing axon and neuron potentials, altering the effect of brain chemical transmitters, and causing random convulsions.

Such power, such a weapon. And because of the subtle influence of the field, those chaotic effects could not be measured directly. The chaos device traveled past the enemy worlds, leaving behind a legacy of corruption both physical and spiritual.

Beq addressed the problem presented by the enemy invasion and bombardment. "Proof is not required in this matter. The evidence is everywhere. Consider the firestorms produced by their falling bombs. Consider the flares of their rocket exhausts boiling away sacred spawning lakes. These point to failure. If not in our mechanicians, then who is at fault?"

"I stake my life on the effectiveness of our detection system. The enemy has produced a new countermeasure that thwarts our most sophisticated equipment. It is you, Beq, you who rank as our leading theoretician, who has failed. You neglected work to float on your ammonia currents and return to a bestial state."

"I have not failed. The enemy need not have contrived new and more diabolical evasion measures." Beq uncurled and rose to the top of the vault. It spread out its body mass to maintain elevation and studied the ruling committee scattered about the rocky chamber. So many of them, so few of any capacity. Beq knew that they *did* blame it.

And perhaps such blame was well directed. Its intellect outclassed theirs. None stood in its rank. Beq pondered how it should have predicted the mechanicians' failure—for it was not possible to come to any other conclusion save that the mechanicians were at fault.

None of the ruling committee understood. And Beq did not understand or appreciate this eons-long war with the enemy. The two cultures did not strive for the same planets. Those worlds favored by the hot-blooded enemy constituted Beq's notion of eternal damnation. It thought that the enemy considered its own fair ammonia wind-wracked planet to be equally unappealing.

So why the war?

Beq did not know. Perhaps a member of the ruling committee had once known, but Beq doubted this. Too many spawnings had passed for that knowledge to be absolute now. Although each division presented added room for mental development, not all knowledge from the parent was carried by each of the spawn-twins. Beq knew that its spawn-twin had certain knowledge of their parent-Beq that it did not possess, but both had inherited the original Beq's mathematical talent—and the oddness that set them apart from all others of their race.

Beq wanted nothing more than to leave this enclosed, constraining chamber and soar on the high-velocity winds far above the surface. When it thinned and let those breezes whip it about the planet, ineffable emotions welled within and promised knowledge unattainable by any other means.

But Beq knew that such comforting thought and stark delight could not occur until this matter of unrestricted bombardment came to a successful conclusion. If the enemy, even at high odds, raided their surface at will, it would be less than a dozen revolutions of the primary before all meaningful life vanished.

Beq tried to imagine the surface heating to the point that water ice melted and those bizarre green things called plants by the enemy began growing. It shrugged off such fantasy. Heat the surface their enemy might. But to actually begin the photosynthesis process that had been discovered in the laboratories? Never. The primary swung through space at such a great distance that the solar constant at the planet's surface was minuscule.

"I will examine the launch area and prove my contention," said Beq. "There has been a serious and vexing mistake made by careless mechanicians."

Beq watched as several others of the ruling committee began their protests. Pride prevented them from analyzing the information available and coming to the same conclusion. It wished it might present the symbolic logic to prove the hypothesis of error but Beq knew this would mean nothing to most of the ruling committee. They lived in another world, and it was not a better one, Beq decided.

It pulled in tentacles finer than mist, solidified, and found an updraft at the side of the cavern. Whistling upward to the frigid surface through a lava chimney, Beq thrilled at the motion. But the instant it erupted into the atmosphere above the surface, Beq's mood turned somber.

Magnesium still burned and an odor both cloying and ugly hung in the air. Beq tried to moderate its gaseous intake from the surrounding contaminated air and failed. It felt sick to the core of its being.

Thinning to an arrow, Beq allowed the wind to take it on a roundabout path to the launch area where it—the parent-Beq—had watched the launching of the first chaos field weapon.

Past the areas melted to slag Beq flew; it knew intense sorrow. What destruction had been wrought on the rugged lava flows that nourished it! Beq did not understand the purpose of this conflict, but it felt no emotion concerning its unleashing of chaos on the fixed form enemy. Any creature who burned and left behind such destruction was not worthy of its pity—or mercy.

Beq tightened its gaseous body into a sphere and plunged downward. Finding a sudden cross current, Beq surged around and through black lava arches ammonia winds had eroded over the centuries. A particularly warm pillar drew it. Beq turned more bulletlike and shot through a tight entry port and into a small cavern populated by a dozen of its kind.

"Beq," greeted a mechanician. "Your spawn-twin . . ."

"Perished," Beq said, cutting off the mechanician's words. It had no desire to linger on personal tragedy. If its questioning uncovered the facts, the ruling committee could correct these mechanicians' errors and such space bombardment would cease. No more of their precious population need die.

"Condolences," said the mechanician.

"Accepted. I wish to study records of the launching."

"Of the chaos field? Or the defense system?"

"The former. The ruling committee already knows of the defense system's failure. It has been thrust upon me to determine why you have not carried out your duties."

"Not so!" protested the mechanician. "We toil diligently!"

"You fail. No other explanation is possible for the enemy's penetration of our system."

"They have new countermeasures that bypass our equipment's detection spectrum," said the mechanician. The sullenness in its voice convinced Beq that the mechanician did not truly believe this.

"The records."

Beq drifted behind the mechanician to a large metal data plate etched with acid. A quick glance satisfied Beq.

"This is incomplete. There are other records. Bring them."

"The other plates have been lost. During the attack. Magnesium has eaten through some and . . ."

The mechanician's voice trailed off. Silence descended on the chamber, leaving only the mournful whine of the ammonia wind whipping in from outside to fill the void. The mechanician knew how feeble this excuse sounded. Both it and Beq knew what had really occurred. No record had been kept—or the records had been purposefully destroyed to prevent punishment for inefficiency.

"Send for *all* records," ordered Beq. It had no desire to serve on the ruling committee, but it would perform its duties well as long as it remained in that position.

The mechanician hurried off so quickly that it left portions of its body behind. Beq rippled and pressurized at such unseemly haste. To weaken the body by such a maneuver usually indicated that a new spawn struggled to recover full control of its functions. For this ancient and unspawned mechanician to do so betold more than inefficiency. Beq began to consider the possibility of severe physical and mental dysfunction in the mechanician.

Beq spent the two planetary revolutions that the mechanician was gone thinking. Its mind manipulated esoteric mathematical concepts, worked on more profound philosophical levels, then erased all from its brain and tried the most simplistic solutions available.

Beq did not like the answer that recurred. No matter what level it tackled the question, an approximation of the same answer provided full explanation.

"Here," said the mechanician, returning with two large plates. It dropped the data into Beq's shadow, a definite breach of etiquette. Beq started to chastise the mechanician, then subsided. A member of the ruling committee might be merciful—and Beq had to admit that the mechanician might not be responsible for its behavior.

Another major ripple, this time accompanied by both pressurization and a flash of reds and greens. Not to be responsible. Beq barely comprehended the enormity of such a concept, yet it was mathematically probable.

It turned to the data plates, computing, comparing the data against its own inherited memory of the chaos field launching, then indulged in wilder speculation. Beq settled around a warm lava pillar made radioactively unstable by application of the chaos field, then began intense calculation.

Beq reconstructed even the most minute detail of the launch. Its own calculations had shown how it was possible for radioactive isotopes to be formed; the direct interaction of field with certain elements produced artificial warmth no less nourishing than that seeping through the crustal plates from the planet's core. But something more now surfaced in Beq's computation.

"The radioactivity cannot be generated indefinitely," it decided. The action of the field with itself produced instability, uncertainty—chaos. The symmetry of radioactive decay and formation could not be supported by the moving field. The probabilities being altered in one direction were also altered in the other. The chance for radioactive decay was changed in precisely the same way that radioactive formation was.

"This violates the concept of chaos," mused Beq. Its equations predicted much. But it had erred in this matter, overlooking higher order solutions to the nonlinear equations. "The field decays because of its own action on space around it," concluded Beq.

It shuddered at this. The launching of the chaos weapon had ruined the surveillance system put into space to defend their planet—and the system had been installed *after* the chaos field had been launched and sent toward the enemy's home world. Residual chaotic effects lingered, ones Beq had not considered.

"I am responsible," it said.

"What? You are the one who allowed the enemy to attack?" demanded the mechanician. "You sabotaged our defenses?"

"No, not directly." Beq still worried over the mechanician's instability of personality and body. Hazy wisps swirled from the mechanician's hintermost tendril. "Were you present at the launching of the field weapon?"

"I was in charge." The mechanician looked like a spawn-parent, almost splitting entirely in half. Only great concentration forced the halves into a coherent whole.

"Are you well?" asked Beq. "Your substance appears thin, as if you require rest and sustenance." How the mechanician could lack for nourishment with the chaotically created radioactive pillar in its workshop was more than Beq could understand—unless the chaos field had worked on the mechanician, turning it into something not quite sane.

"Do you often leave your workshop?" asked Beq.

"I never leave," came the expected answer.

Beq settled and began calculating the residual field effect and how this would translate into erratic behavior in the mechanician. When the results fell out of the intricate and esoteric mathematics, Beq almost turned and caught an updraft to flee.

"This is a dangerous place. The residual chaotic effects are causing great damage, not only to you and your staff, but to everything you manufacture in this chamber."

"The weapon has ruined my defense system?" The mechanician's voice came out thin, high-pitched, unbelieving. "That's not possible. I built well. I am responsible for failure! *I* certified the system. I did. I did!''

Before Beq could issue the words to calm the mechanician, the creature spun through its workshop, whirling about faster and faster until it formed a vortex. Never had Beq seen this, though it had always believed the act possible.

The mechanician killed itself by spinning faster and faster until the radial acceleration overcame the weak intermolecular binding forces holding it in a coherent, thinking, living being. Veils of the creature's being spun away from the core to spread moisture-thin on the chamber's rocky walls.

Beq watched in horror, then calmed. The spectrum of emotion flashing along its gaseous shell faded. Beq realized that death had become commonplace on this world. If the enemy did not kill instantly, then madness did slowly.

Madness Beq had created using the chaos field. Something had altered the flow of energy in the mechanician and caused it to perform aberrant acts. The suicide Beq had just witnessed was only the finale.

What else had the mechanician done? Beq began to study the data plates more intently, trying to understand from what was omitted as much as what had actually been inscribed.

As if liquid helium had been pumped along its ventral side, Beq found what it had feared. The mechanician had made mistake after mistake, then altered the records to hide it. Society had been served when the mechanician had died, Beq realized. But the effects of the chaos field lingered and contaminated planet and population.

Beq finished within four revolutions of the planet about its distant primary, a quick study for the seriousness of the matter. It left the workshop, with the other mechanicians drifting aimlessly, all upset at the loss of their master. Beq neither knew nor cared if those others had been tainted by its creation. The damage had been done. It had loosed a weapon against their enemy—and that weapon had changed like a thing alive, evolving, mutating.

The chaos field did not live, Beq knew. But it changed because of its own nature. It had been constructed and launched to slowly destroy the enemy. It now destroyed itself as it spun through space, changing its internal structure, randomly altering the equations that governed it. Beq no longer predicted the weapon's course or its function. Whatever it did, it did with the full power of chaos behind it.

Beq soared on the ammonia winds, thrilling to the feel. Duty lay in reporting to the ruling committee, but for a moment it could float and soar and experience this animalistic delight.

For a moment. Then Beq, the most able mathematician of an entire race, worked through the intricate symbolic logic that provided answers to profound questions.

Beq understood the mechanician's suicide in that instant of surfacing knowledge. Beq surged higher, body becoming increasingly tenuous and mental responses more primitive. By the time Beq's substance dissipated totally on the upper winds and it joined the mechanician in a newer, higher plane, it had forgotten—almost—about the chaotic horror it had unleashed on the galaxy.

TWO

MICHAEL RALSTON SPUN around in his chair and stared out the small window behind his desk. The peace of the University of Ilium seemed limitless, but Ralston knew that increasingly vicious riots had been raging for days. This lush, green campus only rested before a new bout of unrest seized it.

Ralston reached over and tugged at the mechanical latch on the window, an anachronism that branded him as strange among his peers. Every other professor in the archaeology department had scenic views of mountains or oceans or special displays of far-off worlds to stare at when they daydreamed. Many ordered the scene changed on a daily or weekly basis to duplicate extensive travel. One even insisted that his primary off-world dig sites be displayed so that he could enter his office and be ''inspired'' anew.

Ralston snorted as he thought of Velasquez and the discoveries he'd made on Proteus. A ancient post-spaceflight culture on that planet, yes, but nothing that special. But Velasquez carried the discovery to absurd and pointless heights. To hear him talk, anyone would think that Proteus was *the* discovery of the century.

Ralston fought with the latch and worried the window open on aluminum tracks that galled with every movement and resisted his desire for clean air not from an air conditioner. A soft breeze holding the promise of a mild winter blew in, caught up a miniature tornado of papers on his desk, and further scrambled their order. Ralston ignored this natural refiling. He hiked his feet to the windowsill and tried to relax.

"Dammit," he muttered. "Velasquez *hasn't* made the discovery of the century. *I* have!" Ralston folded arms across his broad chest and tossed back his head, moving an annoying lock of hair from his eyes. The work he'd done under time pressures in the Alpha system constituted major discoveries on a dozen different fronts. The Alphans had been a pre-space culture propelled into sublight star travel to escape the plague of chaos that had touched their planet.

Either the Alphans' escape to the Beta system *or* the disruption of their culture due to the passage of the chaos device should have firmly established Ralston's career. The death of a graduate student on Alpha had brought only notoriety and censure—and no fame. By the time Ralston had smoothed over the trouble with the University and the student's influential family and returned to Alpha, the pre-nova condition in the system's primary had progressed too far.

The star exploded, Ralston and his students and the solar observers escaping only hours before. Nels Bernssen had become a shining light in astrophysics because of his observations. Ralston had been ignored, even though his work had uncovered an Alphan telepathic device used in their museums for teaching purposes. His most promising graduate student's father now controlled development and marketing of the device for the University. Dr. Michael Ralston did not figure in Leonid Disa's plans, academically or otherwise.

Ralston sighed. As for his graduate student, Leonore Disa, she and Nels Bernssen would soon be married. She had successfully written and defended her thesis and had earned her doctorate, in spite of the sorry reputation of her advisor.

For that, Ralston was happy. Leonore deserved her degree and the stature due her in archaeology. Her work had been exemplary. Her advisor's problems with the University chancellor, the others in the archaeology department, and the campus in general shouldn't reflect badly on her.

Still, Ralston felt cheated. Everyone prospered and he languished in disgrace. Leonore had her degree. Bernssen had become a celebrity from formulating his Bernssen Condition for Stellar Instability. And a university mathematician, Westcott, had more data from the chaos device than he could analyze in a lifetime of work.

The chaos device.

"Dammit!" shouted Ralston. His feet fell to the floor and he bent forward, chin on crossed arms as he stared across the campus Quadrangle. The chaos device had been his discovery—and it was the most significant archaeological discovery of all time. Was it a weapon gone awry? Was it an attempt to communicate that had proven more dangerous than informative? What was it?

What?

Every chance for investigation of the device had been ripped away from him. The Alpha primary had gone nova, destroying all evidence of the device's passage through that system. The Beta system's primary showed Bernssen Condition Instability; that sun would soon explode and erase all evidence of the device's passage.

"Hell and damnation, I can't even convince Chancellor Salazar that the University ought to help the people on Beta 7." Ralston had found not only the remains of the Alphan refugees on Beta 5 but also evidence of other colonization. The gas giant Beta 7 had proved the home for those creatures, more fluid than material—and of truly alien concerns. They knew that their star's lifetime was measured in short years. And they did not care. The being responsible for the colonization was considered insane for unsocial activities of experimentation, inquiry and exploration of other planets, construction of satellite bases.

"Too many alien races to aid, Salazar says," grumbled Ralston. "Can't afford it now. Hell, let him take one percent of what he and Disa make off the telepathic projector and they could finance the start of an evacuation program."

Ralston stopped mumbling, knowing that this wasn't possible. Evacuating an entire culture—and one so physically and mentally alien—proved beyond the resources of any world, much less a single university. But Ralston hated the callous attitude shown by Salazar and the others. In part it came from their dislike for him. Repeatedly, they had denied him tenure. With Velasquez back from his easy excavation on Proteus 4, the chancellor would see to removing Ralston permanently from the faculty. The only thing that had stopped Salazar previously was the lack of qualified personnel to teach.

"Cancel even one class," said Ralston to himself in a mocking, sarcastic tone, "and the department loses precious grant money. And that casts a bad light on everyone in the University community." Keeping Ralston on had proven financially advantageous. Firing him immediately and cancelling the three courses he taught would have cost the archaeology department grants equal to a full third of their trivial annual budget for research.

Ralston jerked around when his message terminal beeped that mail awaited his attention. He reached over and began digging in the stacks of old books and papers that hadn't been moved by the wind gusting through the window. He located the computer terminal and quickly scanned the message flashing on the screen.

"About time," he said. Ralston had submitted a survey paper to the *Novo Terra Journal of Field Archaeology* covering the impact of the chaos device on the Alphan culture, how it had induced a mass insanity and brought about epileptic seizures. With it accepted, Ralston felt confident that a series on the Alphans could be run.

Only now did he have the time to sift through the photos of their ruins, the computer data about the artifacts found, their distribution and importance—and the all-important telepathic projection equipment discovered in the subterranean museum. Ralston had a lifetime of papers to write and had just scratched the surface.

"Let's see when they'll publish." With the *Journal*'s reputation for promptness, he hoped to see it on the network before the end of the month. Ralston smiled as he pressed the "accept" button to signal willingness to read the message.

The smile faded as Ralston scanned the rejection. At first, he thought it was a terrible joke. Bernssen had been known to play pranks. Maybe Leonore had helped him with access codes. Ralston read the message again and found the verification number. No matter how elaborate Bernssen got with his sophomoric practical jokes, he'd be hard-pressed to fake one of this magnitude.

Ralston knew that the journal rejection was real long seconds before the computer verified transmission from the publication office. Ralston swept some of the books from the keyboard and began tapping in an angry response. Almost instantly came the reply.

Ralston didn't know which he hated worse. The speed of the answer told him that someone gleefully awaited his protest. That was bad. What Ralston came to realize was the ultimate in professional assassination was a refereed journal refusing his work, not because of anything wrong with his paper but because it had been Michael Ralston submitting it.

"Go on, give me a hearing," he said savagely as he filled in the exception request on the computer. Ralston snapped the terminal off when the exception was noted and rejected, again almost instantaneously.

They had cut him off in all directions, and there was nothing he could do about it. Chancellor Salazar didn't have to grant tenure, especially if no one spoke strongly in Ralston's favor. The journal didn't have to accept his paper unless the "impartial" referee approved it as being original work of a professional quality.

Ralston's finest discoveries were being reburied because no one approved of him personally.

Ralston spun around and glowered at the peaceful campus, as if accusing it of originating his problems. In a way, it only reflected the world Ralston had come to hate so much. He enjoyed teaching; he hated the petty bureaucrats in administration. Nothing thrilled Ralston more than digging at a site, finding secrets of civilizations long dead, and returning their glory to the full sight of interested scholars. But the delight he took in such discovery dimmed when he dealt with the politics of tenure and publication.

He could protest. The system allowed that. But Ralston knew it'd do him little good. The very people listening to his complaints were the ones responsible for them.

Ralston knew it would be a long, long time until he headed another expedition. And he had to! The chaos device swung through the galaxy on a trajectory calculated by Westcott from the archaeological information. That device had to be studied. It had destroyed countless suns through induced chaotic instability. Ralston knew of two cultures it had either destroyed or soon would. The Alphans had died out to the last being. The Betans on their gas giant world, so different from Alphan or human, would soon follow.

Had there already been Gammas and Deltas and Epsilons? More? How many intelligent beings had perished because of the synaptic disruption that was the chaos device's illegitimate legacy?

Ralston chafed that he'd not get the opportunity to study the device for information about the race that had constructed it—and Betan observations had confirmed that it was, indeed, artificial. Why would any society build such a device?

Ralston had to know. He had to.

Ralston walked across the deserted Quadrangle, hands jammed deep into pockets. In the distance he heard the loudspeakers at work whipping student radicals into a frenzy. He shook his head. He knew the source of that unrest. It wasn't the students' fault as much as it was the single P'torra who always lurked near the edge of those riots, impulse driver in hand. The constantly striving P'torra used the computer device to assay the emotions and emotional potential of a crowd, then carefully manipulated the factors feeding the unrest. A deft P'torra might be able to bring an entire city to the point of anarchy—and most humans refused to believe this.

Ralston knew. Only too well, he knew. He had fought in the Nex-P'torra war on the side of the reptilian Nex rather than with the humanoid P'torra. That was another bone of contention on campus. For all their vaunted open-mindedness, few of the professors were willing to be seen with non-humanoid aliens. Ralston had tried to assure them that the Nex were more like humans psychologically than the P'torra, but outward shape mattered more to those bigots.

Ralston had seen the planets laid waste by the P'torra bio-weapons. He could never align himself with a race capable of such emotionless genocide.

The sound of speeches reached a crescendo, then faded. Ralston tried not to strain to hear what was being said. He knew most of it by heart. The lone P'torra on campus had directed more than one crowd against Ralston in the past months, more for practice than out of true malice. Ralston wasn't even sure the P'torra had emotions—certainly they lacked compassion and love and other feelings Ralston counted as necessary for a human to be truly human.

He pushed the thought of the humanoid aliens from his mind and found that he kept returning to the rejected scientific paper. Ralston wasn't sure which he preferred to seethe about the most. The journal rejecting his work simply because it had been Dr. Michael Ralston who had submitted it cut deep into pride and ego and the need to inform others of the danger brought by the chaos device.

But the P'torra had been more active and it would only be a matter of time before the alien turned the rioting against him personally, if for no other reason just because he was here and a known opponent from a war long declared a stalemate.

"What's the old saying?" he wondered aloud, trying to remember what a medieval literature professor friend of his sometimes said. "Nuking fish in a pond. That's how hard it will be to get rid of me. If Salazar doesn't do it first, the P'torra definitely will."

Ralston stopped and stared at the building he had unconsciously walked toward. The laboratory building stood silent, classes over for most students who actually attended the University to use the expensive lab equipment. Ralston sighed. Most of his students had chosen the transmission option, preferring to stay at their homes and watch his lectures via satellite link. Only those in lab courses routinely attended now, even though Ralston wished all would physically attend. Something about the actual bodily presence of students inspired him to put more into his lectures than if he simply spoke to a flat, cold, gray electroceramic camera eye.

But this building housed Westcott's lab. Ralston didn't like Westcott—that understated his feelings. He disliked the man intensely and, if Ralston had an honest instant, admitted to fearing him. Ralston went inside and climbed the stairs to Westcott's second-floor lab. He paused uncertainly outside the battered wood door with the red sign ordering everyone away.

He didn't want to talk to Westcott. If he never saw the man

again it'd be a century too soon, but Ralston recognized within him the need for some human contact.

If talking with Westcott could be called human contact. If Westcott could be called human, he mused.

Ralston took a long, deep, calming breath and found it did nothing to still his racing pulse. The last time he had barged into Westcott's lab, he had found himself floating endlessly between the stars, cut off from gravity and sight and all reality. Westcott had reduced unwanted sensory input so that he could listen to data turned into musical tones, seeking the proper relationship aurally rather than visually. Ralston opened the door, peered in, and saw a dim light, which was all Westcott ever tolerated, but no fantastic stellar display.

He went in, still cautious.

Westcott sat hunched over a table, arms thrown limply on the surface. Three different computer screens were turned so that Westcott sat in the center of this electronic spiderweb. Ralston's eyes immediately traced across the room to a large computer with a single infrared communications link atop it. The baleful red of the com-link told that Westcott was connected directly to the computer, the artificial circuitry imbedded in his head translating the superspeed input into slower terms Westcott's brain could handle.

Ralston held back the shudder of distaste. Few people were given permits authorizing the surgery that directly linked them to a computer. Westcott's framed license hung on the wall, the only decoration visible in the dreary lab.

Ralston avoided walking through the IR linkage. Westcott always complained that interruption of data flow gave him a headache. Ralston stood and waited for the mathematician to notice him; something that might take hours if Westcott was engaged in complex equations.

Almost immediately, though, Westcott looked up, his eyes slightly glazed as if he'd been taking drugs. Ralston knew better. The only reason Westcott would ever indulge was to speed up the computer-mind communication, and Westcott had said repeatedly that drugs dulled the edge, not sharpened it. The cause turning Westcott's face slack lay within the total isolation from reality. Westcott forgot the world around him and lived only within the speed-of-light constraints of the computer's immense memory.

"Pretty," said Ralston, indicating all three screens. "I don't recognize the patterns. Did you create them?"

"Chaos," murmured Westcott. "Those are the colors of chaos."

"What?"

"I needed some method for watching how the equations vary when I make small changes in a single parameter. The colors change, making the effect obvious."

"Oh." Ralston knew that the intricate chaos equations Westcott had mastered permitted no deviation in boundary conditions. The slightest change might bring about catastrophic results—hence the name "chaotic." A system of nonlinear differential equations could be set up deterministically describing a thundercloud—and the beating of a single butterfly's wing at the edge could produce lightning by introducing a new parameter.

What Westcott studied was the flap of such a wing.

"The colors tell you how fast the equations go to infinity?" asked Ralston.

"Yes, hmm, yes," said Westcott, his eyes focusing on Ralston. The archaeologist wished the man would turn his attention elsewhere. Those eyes carried more than the seeds of madness within their depths.

"I use complex numbers in my equations, then take the sine of the number. Then I take the sine of that and plot it, then take sine of the result and if it is different, assign another color."

"If not?"

"The same color. It is possible for entire planes to be equivalent in my mapping schemes. But these, these are the ones of interest. The speed at which they diverge to infinity—or converge—tells me much."

Ralston knew that Westcott had made a reputation for himself in both physics and mathematics circles by accurately predicting which nucleus of a forty atom sample of uranium would decay. With this specific solution of the chaos equations, Westcott never missed. Radioactive decay had become predictable under stringent laboratory conditions. Ralston only vaguely understood the furor in quantum physics this created. Indeterminacy was being questioned, but Westcott had gone beyond this, ignoring critics, ignoring supporters, concentrating on newer and more intricate solutions to the equations.

Westcott mastered chaos slowly, turning it into a slave for the first time.

"For the second time," Ralston said to himself. "Whoever launched the chaos device knew how to . . ."

"The builders might have been lucky. It might be accidental."

"Do your equations prove this?"

"No, not really. Just a guess, a speculation. Too much has been happening. Look, look at this plot. I alternately take the sine and tangent of the complex number $z = 1 + 7i$ and plot those colors. It reveals much about the internal working of the device that has wrecked the stellar fusion mechanisms in the stars."

"It does?" Ralston stared at the pretty colors marching across the screen. They reminded him of Rorschach patterns more than anything else, but to Westcott they provided answers.

"Can you build a chaos device of your own?"

"No, that's beyond me, but the mathematics of it are becoming accessible. I understand more. A bit here, a bit there. I will soon understand it all."

Ralston didn't ask what happened when he did. Westcott's mind would turn to even stranger paths of knowledge, paths never imagined just a few short years earlier. Just a few hours earlier than Ralston's discoveries in the Alpha system of the chaos field and its effect on an entire society.

His anger mounted once more. Bernssen prospered. Leonore Disa got her degree. Westcott became even more renown in his field. The University got the use of the telepathic projector. Everyone but Michael Ralston profited from his discoveries!

Even worse, Ralston had to make them understand that the danger presented by the chaos device might transcend anything that had ever confronted mankind before.

Suns going nova, people developing epilepsy, brains malfunctioning, DNA patterns becoming confused and creating uncontrollable mutations—what else? The dangers screamed at him and no one listened. The others were too caught up in their fame and good fortune to listen to an intellectual pariah.

"Keep me informed of your progress," Ralston said. He could no longer stand the sight of Westcott and his shaved head with the IR probe obscenely protruding from the pate. He wasn't even sure he could stand himself. He had tried to touch some humanity in Westcott and failed, as he always had. Whether the failure rested on Westcott or himself, Ralston wasn't sure.

He wasn't even sure he cared.

Not with the universe in danger from the chaos device orbiting through the Orion spiral arm—where all known civilizations were clustered.

THREE

MICHAEL RALSTON CLOSED the lab door behind him with a click that sounded like a thunderclap of doom. He leaned back against the cool, varnished wood surface, sweat running in cold, itching rivers down his spine.

"Why?" he wondered out loud. Ralston had no easy answer for that question—no answer at all. He had been through so much and had profited little from it. What rewards that had come his way turned out to be insubstantial and even philosophical. Leonore Disa did well and prospered. Seeing a student succeed made him glow with achievement of a job well done. But Ralston couldn't deny that Leonore would have done well in any field she'd chosen. The daughter of one of the richest men on Novo Terra would never end up begging over the charity broadcasts.

Ralston heaved himself forward and took a deep, steadying breath. Feeling sorry for himself accomplished nothing. He wanted to rewrite the article he'd sent in to the *Journal* and see if another might take it. Salazar and the others couldn't have blacklisted him everywhere. If nothing else, a popularization might be good for the tri-vid. It had all the elements that amused the masses. Dying races, peril, derring-do. Ralston smiled as he thought of casting himself as the intrepid professor leading his stalwart band of investigators into the dangers found in the Alpha and Beta systems.

"If I don't stand a chance as professor, why not give acting a try?" The outrageous idea amused him so much that he

whistled a bawdy song off-key by the time he descended the
stairs and reached the side entrance to the laboratory building.

The whistling stopped when he heard the chants of the
crowd. Ralston slipped behind a large pillar and looked around
it cautiously. Some distance away a student stood on a make-
shift dais and harangued his peers. The words rang clear and
brittle. The hatred never stopped, even after the war had
sputtered to an indecisive halt. Ralston considered this the
major problem in the Nex-P'torra conflict's outcome. Neither
side had won decisively. This left uncertainty in both the
combatants and curious onlookers about who was "right,"
and it planted a seed of hatred to blossom again over the same
issues.

Ralston had fought beside the reptilian Nex. He'd do so
again, for the same reasons.

He felt the hairs on the back of his neck begin to rise at an
unwanted presence behind him. Ralston turned and saw a
P'torra standing a hundred meters away, stubby fingers working swiftly over the keys of the impulse driver resting in the
broad palm of his hand. The professor didn't think the alien
had seen him. The P'torra concentrated too hard on the input
to his miniature psychological evaluator. The alien came to a
decision, reached up, and spoke softly into the microphone
concealed under a wrinkled lapel.

Ralston jerked around, eyes narrowed and intense. The
leader of the demonstration continued his harangue but the
mood of the crowd changed subtly. If Ralston hadn't known
of the P'torra's prompting, he would have thought that the
students had simply reached the boiling point on their own.
That the P'torra had signaled the speaker told Ralston more.
The P'torra had found the precise trigger to incite violence.

Ralston watched it erupt before his eyes. Captivated, almost hypnotized by the intensity of the riot, Ralston found
himself following the mob of students across the Quadrangle
and toward the administration building. Seeing their destination, Ralston hurried ahead, taking a shortcut that brought
him into the long hallway leading to Chancellor Salazar's
office.

Ralston skidded to a halt on the highly polished floor when
he saw that he hadn't acted swiftly enough to warn the

chancellor of the danger coming through his front doors. The students burst inside and smashed through the double doors leading to Salazar's office. Ralston slid into a doorway and watched.

There was nothing he could do, and in any case, he saw no reason to risk his life for Salazar's. If anything, his sentiments matched those of the students chanting for Salazar's resignation. The only drawback lay in the source of their desire. Ralston knew it came not from within themselves or out of shock and indignation at Salazar's policies but from the P'torra and his damnable computer.

Ralston recognized Salazar's secretary as the crowd tossed him from side to side. The man tried to escape but too many hands groped for him, each seeking another drop of blood, a tiny scratch of skin, a piece of clothing. Sobbing, the man fell to his knees. Ralston saw in that act a mistake that could mean his life.

The leader harshly commanded a small group to take the secretary away. They kicked and pommeled him before jerking him to his feet. The man stumbled a few paces; not wanting to wait for him to rise, they dragged him away, not caring that he bled from a dozen minor wounds or held his arm as if it had been severely injured.

Ralston heard the student leader's demands.

"Deal with us, Dr. Salazar, or you'll deal with history! We demand redress for all the evils committed by the University."

Ralston had no idea what evils these might be—probably imagined or even created by the P'torra. The University of Ilium had a reputation of being conservative and not a little cowardly when it came to facing difficult political decisions. His own problems with Salazar showed that the preferred solution was flight or subterfuge.

The professor slipped along the corridor, his click-click steps drowned out by the students' angry cries. Outside the administration building once more, Ralston circled and found the group of four students bullying Salazar's secretary. The four took turns beating the man. Ralston knew what good sense dictated. He should walk away, find a com unit, and summon the campus security force.

If he wanted to feel he was in some way getting back at

Salazar for sabotaging his career, he could let the pompous
ass of a secretary take his licks and find some consolation in
this.

Ralston did neither. Salazar ran from his problems or tried
to get rid of them, never squarely facing anything of a
complex moral nature. Ralston was of a different bent. He
had to act.

One student's balled fist rose to descend on the side of the
secretary's bloodied face. Ralston acted instinctively. His
fingers closed around the young man's wrist, went along with
the force of the blow, redirecting it only at the last possible
instant. The fist missed the secretary's head—and sent the
student stumbling facedown to the ground. Ralston didn't
bother warning the other three.

He spun and kicked at a kneecap. The sudden yielding
under his feet told him he'd broken the cartilage and need
worry no more about this opponent. A short punch to the
belly doubled over another. The remaining student came in
from behind. Ralston drove his elbow back as hard as he
could and impacted hard on the man's lowest rib. The jolt
rocked Ralston forward even as it stunned the student.

Ralston recovered first. A fist driven into an exposed throat
ended the fight.

Ralston looked around, a faint smile on his lips. He took
no pleasure in fighting, especially when the others presented
no real challenge. But they had shown no honor in ganging
up on the secretary. The man lay on the ground, crying
piteously.

"Are you all right?" Ralston asked. He turned the man
over and probed with merciless fingers. The secretary winced
but his reaction was one of anger, not pain. Nothing except
for his right arm had been broken or even much damaged.

"Verd, I'm alive. Not much more." The man straightened
painfully, then saw his rescuer. "You, I might have known,"
the secretary gasped between split lips. Blood trickled down
his chin. He wiped it away, cringing at the pain this caused.
"You're responsible. You sent them in to get me!"

Arguing would do no good. The man was Salazar's lackey.
Let him think what he wanted. Ralston hadn't rescued him
intending to get into Salazar's good graces. The secretary had

been in trouble and for that reason alone Ralston had risked his own safety to aid him. Honor didn't require any more of Ralston.

He stood and peered down at the battered man. "The campus security will be here soon. I'm sure Salazar has alerted them, unless the crowd's managed to disrupt the com system."

Ralston didn't think that an impulsive riot would show such planning. After all, the P'torra merely flexed his muscles to see how far he could manipulate. The success or failure of the students and their protest meant nothing to him.

"I'll have you in remand for this, Ralston. I swear it! You're the one responsible for them doing this to me. They're only doing what you ordered them to do!"

Ralston walked away without turning back. Let the man think what he wanted. To Ralston it made no difference. His tenure at the University had been denied and they could dismiss him for any reason. Even with tenure, he wasn't sure that Salazar couldn't come up with adequate rationale to fire him.

"You need not have intruded into this exercise," came a soft voice that made Ralston spin about. The P'torra stood behind a waist-high bush of late-flowering thorny pyracantha. Ralston considered reaching out and grabbing the P'torra by the lapel— the one concealing the microphone—and pulling him face-first into the sharp spines. The P'torra seemed to understand the risk and stepped back.

"I shouldn't have meddled," Ralston agreed. "But sometimes a man has to make a stand. This was a minor one."

"He is not worth your effort."

Again Ralston had to agree. "However, any effort against you is worthwhile."

"Your attitude is one I find hard to fathom." The P'torra pulled his impulse driver from a pouch at his belt. Fat, stubby fingers flew across the keys. What data went in or what results flashed on the tiny screen Ralston didn't know.

"How much longer are you going to incite the riots? I'd think burning down a building or two would be enough. Or must you kill a few administrators before your 'exercise' is finished?"

"Such bitterness, but then this is to be expected from
you." The P'torra widened his stance and settled into what
Ralston considered a defensive posture. To physically attack a
P'torra required more than bare hands. The thick layer of
subcutaneous fat insulated them from both temperature ex-
tremes and assault. A long, thin knife blade such as he'd
carried as a soldier for the Nex would have worked nicely. Or
even a more sophisticated sidearm.

"Interesting," said the P'torra, blunt fingers still working
on the keys. "There seems to be no convenient verbal lever
to employ against you."

Ralston started to agree, then bit back the words. The
P'torra played on the sense of moral superiority Ralston felt
over the alien. Any advantage for exploitation would be used.
Any.

"There are levers in every human," said Ralston.

The P'torra smiled, thick lips rippling. He replaced the
impulse driver in its pouch and said, "You are correct. All
humans have emotions, and those emotions can be molded
into patterns more in keeping with P'torra goals. It is difficult
to maintain the level of involvement, however. You creatures
have such a transient attention span."

"You mean we don't stay brainwashed."

"I am unfamiliar with this term, 'brainwashed.' "

"An old one from Earth describing what you're attempt-
ing." Ralston tried to decide if the P'torra had given him
worthwhile information. Was he saying that the P'torra, once
swayed, could not easily revert to their prior belief? It had
always perplexed Ralston why the P'torra expended so much
effort briefly altering human opinion. The P'torra might not
be able to understand why their procedures worked for only
short periods. Playing on emotion worked—until the emotion
changed.

"What are you going to do with Chancellor Salazar?"

"I? I will do nothing with him. In fact, I have nothing
against the man, in the sense you imply. It might surprise you
to know that I have seen only pictures of him and have done
nothing in the way of research about his policies. My project
depends on isolated responses. Can I generate appropriate
action from a limited number of stimuli. Actually patterning

my programs on Dr. Salazar's record would introduce a variable I have no wish to correct for."

"Then all the rioting is purely academic?"

The P'torra's shoulders weren't designed for shrugging. He shuddered all over in a gesture Ralston equated with a shrug. "What else? I have no true desire to be on this filthy world of yours. Only to seek knowledge do I come here."

"When will the P'torra start a war against us?"

"Again, such bitterness. It comes from associating with slime creatures. They have affected your outlook on the universe, Dr. Ralston. You should choose your comrades more carefully."

The tone made Ralston even more cautious. He read into it a warning that had nothing to do with his past association with the Nex.

"You have nothing to fear from us," the P'torra went on. "We come only in peace." The smile this time revealed twin rows of needle-sharp teeth. The P'torra relaxed his defensive posture and waddled off in the direction of the administration building. The sound of security sirens filled the air, and the P'torra had work to do, things to learn, humans to manipulate.

Ralston idly rubbed a skinned knuckle across his shirt as he watched the P'torra cross the grassy area in front of the administration building. The veiled threat made little sense. Ralston shrugged it off. This might be nothing more than another verbal assault dictated by the P'torra's impulse driver, though Ralston had a deep-down feeling it was something more. He had no time to worry over such things.

He had classes to prepare for. A paper to rewrite. People to contact. If Salazar wanted rid of him, somewhere else on Novo Terra there must be a position that would allow him to continue his study of the chaos device.

More than the immediate threat posed by the P'torra, the chaos field or device or weapon—no matter how he thought of it—presented a world threat unparalleled in history. It had destroyed the Alphans, bringing about epileptic seizures in the people and stellar instability in an otherwise ordinary star.

The Betans would soon follow, dying in the hot embrace of their sun's explosion. Who else? How many other races had already died? How many more would perish because Ralston couldn't get anyone at the University to believe that this was a significant menace, something worthy of intense study?

The feelings of impotence returned.

Hands thrust into his pockets, Ralston walked aimlessly, unconsciously turning away from the loud noises of the crowd and the whine of security force sirens. He no longer had the morbid curiosity about the fate of Salazar and the others. If anything, he might find himself brought up on criminal charges when the beaten secretary gave his statement. Ralston had passed the point of caring.

All he wanted was to do archaeology. He had made the most significant finds of the century—perhaps of all time— and had garnered no recognition for it. He had to live off what sense of achievement he had inside. Worst of all, there was more work to do, exciting, fulfilling work.

The threat of the chaos device aside, who had built it? When? What was its purpose? What sort of being sent such a machine among the stars? Ralston wondered if it might be a mode of communication rather than a weapon of war. Different cultures saw menace in different things, communication in still others.

The Onslong culture of Gamma Triangulus 3 declared war by spraying scent into the air. The first human ambassadors had inadvertently started a war by wearing the wrong perfumes. One chameleon race Ralston had read about attached great importance to skin color. No human had been able to negotiate trade treaties with them because the coloration was wrong; however, scientific information was freely exchanged because the coloration was acceptable for this purpose.

Perhaps the chaos device wasn't even intended as a communique. It might have been built for some other purpose. But Ralston would never be able to study it and the machinery powering it without a fully funded expedition.

He heaved a deep sigh thinking that Leonid Disa might be the only available source of money for such a trip. Ralston hated dealing with the man. Interstellar Computronics hadn't become one of the largest corporations on Novo Terra without a sharp eye kept on profits. Anything funded by Disa through IC would become the company's property. The joint venture with the University on the telepathic projector showed Disa's astuteness in such matters. Ralston wondered how badly Salazar had lost out on that deal.

The very nature of the physical law-confusing properties of the chaos field made it dangerous to anyone contemptuous of its power. Leonid Disa was contemptuous of any power other than his own. Ralston had seen enough of the man to know this. It amazed the professor that the magnate's daughter had turned out to be so earnest and forthright in pursuing knowledge for its own sake. Leonore's need to unravel the mysteries of the past for the sheer job of *knowing* elevated her far above her father, as far as Ralston was concerned.

He'd ask Disa to fund the expedition only if there was no other way. And then Ralston would begin to make plans to destroy any information that might be exploited before it became dangerous.

Any device altering the chance properties of weather or radioactive decay or the stellar fusion process or even the way a human's mind functioned was not to be taken lightly.

Ralston stopped on a low hill and looked out over the campus. It had again become deceptively calm in the twilight. The riot had been successfully quelled, from the chancellor's viewpoint, Ralston guessed, in that no students were to be seen. This unrest could only lend impetus to those on the Committee on Academics wanting to conduct all classes via tri-vid and keep students off campus entirely.

Ralston shook his head. Lab courses were pale and second-rate when conducted for the students. Even with clever placement of the cameras, having the professor perform the experiments wasn't the same as hands-on experience for the student. Beyond this, Ralston preferred his students to be physically present in a classroom. It might be archaic but the interaction seemed more intense. The mere act of coming to the classroom also showed a modicum of dedication that wasn't there when a student need only turn on his set and watch from a tiny cubicle, perhaps halfway around the planet.

The professor knew all this was moot, at least as far as he was concerned. His career teaching at the University of Ilium had ended on a sour note.

Ralston sat down on the grass, noting how it had begun turning brown as winter's first breezes touched it. The sunset

was particularly vivid, the high cirrus clouds catching the
pink and purple along their feathery ice crystals.

The sunlight faded rapidly. Ralston decided he had much in
common with it. His star was setting, too, and chilly winter
was coming on. It would be a harsh battle from now on, away
from the comforting cloister of academe.

But it was a battle that had to be fought. Michael Ralston
had never turned away before from a fight for what he
considered right. He wouldn't now.

He stood and brushed off the dried grass before starting
down the hill. Less than halfway down, he paused, head
cocked to one side. Something or someone moved through
the bushes less then ten meters away.

He sniffed the air, trying to pick up the P'torra scent. Only
crisp autumn smells found their way to his nose. More curious than apprehensive, Ralston moved along the path until he
came to a tree with large overhanging branches. He never
broke stride as he reached up and caught the thick lower limb
and pulled himself upward. Many of the leaves had already
fallen; this proved both a boon and a hindrance.

Although the leaves rustled dryly and gave scant protection
from probing eyes, the sparseness allowed him to make his
way along the limb without much noise. Ralston came to the
end of the limb and dropped to his belly, arms and legs
dangling. He waited.

For a few minutes, Ralston thought his senses had betrayed
him, that he'd become too nervous over the encounter with
the P'torra and the rioting students. Then came small slithering
noises that told him something did follow.

Closely.

Ralston prepared to drop from the limb as the sound came
ever closer in the darkness.

FOUR

A HISSING NOISE, hardly louder than the wind blowing through the upper leaves of the tree, reached Michael Ralston's ears. He tensed. The sound was a familiar one to him.

Ralston swung off the tree limb and dropped lightly to the ground, staying in a crouch. "Where are you?" he whispered.

The hissing came from his right. Ralston pivoted and stared directly into two peculiarly irised yellow eyes that burned with fanatical intensity. Ralston reached out slowly, his right hand palm up and fingers spread wide. A long black, forked tongue flicked out and damply touched each of his fingertips, then stroked roughly across his palm, sampling, scenting.

"Much time it has been, Ralston doctor."

Ralston stood slowly. A dark figure shot forward with incredible speed, brushed over his legs, and rose until the reptilian face behind those eyes was only a centimeter from his.

"Commander Slenth," greeted Ralston. "It's been over five years since I've seen you."

Ralston realized how much he had become reintegrated into human society when he recoiled slightly from the Nex when Slenth thrust out his own hand, palm up and slender, taloned fingers spread wide. Ralston swallowed hard and covered his surprise as he bent down and repeated the greeting given him. The alien's hand tasted slightly alkaline, but it was a flavor Ralston had come to tolerate during his tenure with the Nex fighting forces.

"Your tongue is wet and your courage high," Ralston said ritualistically.

"Danger leaps every spot about here," said Slenth. Ralston had expected an equally formal reply. That he didn't receive it constituted a major breach of Nex honor—unless Slenth's appraisal of the danger was accurate.

"What? The P'torra?"

"P'torra fish," the Nex agreed, adding the insult with some enthusiasm.

"We can go to my office and talk."

The Nex hesitated, then bobbed his slender head rapidly. Ralston swallowed again, realizing how comfortable he had become teaching at Ilium, seeing only his own species. Everything about the Nex struck him as odd now, alien and—evil. The thin-boned skull and close-set yellow eyes reminded him of desert lizards on burned-out Earth. Although the Nex stood less than shoulder high on Ralston, a long tail swished restlessly behind the muscled body. Taking that powerful appendage into account, the Nex would stretch longer than any two men of normal height. Slender arms almost laughably weak waved about wildly to show the true level of the reptile's consternation and the strong legs set Slenth to bouncing up and down.

Ralston wasn't sure how even a mother could love this brown-scaled reptilian nightmare. The dread and even fear inspired in most humans at the sight of the Nex were understandable and their inability to learn human syntax as well as the P'torra made the differences between the two races even more apparent.

Ralston paused for a moment. The Nex weren't as vocal as the P'torra because they depended on more primitive senses and their thought processes were markedly different. The greeting ritual was based more on scent and taste—virtually the same for a reptile—than word inflection and tone. The thrill of fear that had coursed through Ralston died down as he remembered the other things about the Nex, the reasons he had fought beside them.

Shape and sensory input had nothing to do with kindness and caring and, in spite of their outward appearance, true humanity. In the ways that counted most, the Nex were more human and humane than the diabolical P'torra.

"All places, the P'torra travel here. Must danger look out always," Slenth said.

"We're safe enough," said Ralston. "The P'torra spent the day causing riots. He'll be safely in his tank analyzing the results." Still, the professor kept a wary eye on any student he saw. Luckily, the campus security force had swept through and chased off most of the students. The Quadrangle lay cloaked in shadow and a silence both palpable and intimidating.

"Much more danger to me. To us," Slenth insisted. The reptile shrugged sloping shoulders to get his harness into place. Ralston noticed for the first time that Slenth's clothing concealed several flat energy packs. He failed to find the nozzles for the energy weapons those modules powered.

For Slenth to come into human society armed in this fashion told Ralston much. Slenth, like all Nex, observed human laws and mores scrupulously. No matter what indignities were heaped on him, the Nex stoically endured them, realizing that not everyone could accept him or his race easily. Unless Slenth had changed drastically in the years since Ralston had served with him, the Nex would never consider violence a way to settle a dispute with a human.

"Do you plan to use the weapon?" Ralston asked.

"If necessary. Many occurrences strangely happen often and dangerous to us recently."

Ralston wished he could speak Nex and eliminate the problems with deciphering all Slenth said, but two long years of attempts had availed him little. Only the most rudimentary Nex speech sounds could be reproduced by the clumsy human solid tongue. Slenth's delicate forked tongue darted out and both tips vibrated to produce a buzzing noise that Ralston recognized as one of intense impatience. Whatever bothered Slenth was not trivial in nature.

"In here." Ralston motioned toward the side door that led to a broad marble stairway spiraling around to the second floor where his office looked out over the Quad. Slenth tested the air with his sensitive tongue again, garnering scents and checking for danger. Only when his thin head bobbed quickly did Ralston go up the stairs. He trusted Slenth with his life. If the Nex sensed no danger, none would be waiting at the top of the stairs.

And none was. Each of Ralston's footsteps echoed hollowly down the deserted corridor. Slenth came behind, his footfalls gliding, making only small scratching noises as talons tapped into the hard flooring. Ralston went into his office and said, "Lights, minimum."

The computer obediently turned on the lights and kept them at a level that barely cast shadows. Ralston closed down the polarizer on the window to prevent anyone from across the Quad from seeing Slenth.

"Well?" asked Ralston. "You've come to ask a favor of me. What is it?"

"Humans eager worst to think of Nex. Cannot friends of old seek out others of same time?"

"That's not so, at least in my case, Slenth. You know that. Didn't we fight alongside each other in dozens of battles as comrades?" Ralston leaned back in his chair, eyes half closed as he remembered. The Nex preferred physical confrontation while the P'torra were more devious. The P'torra might infect an entire planet's population with their bio-weapons, but the Nex mind concentrated on frontal assaults, definite battles with precisely defined strategic outcomes. The Nex fleet had landed shock troops on many planets, and on scores of battlefields he and Slenth had fought side by side, sometimes victorious, many times not.

The P'torra had been successful in their use of impulse drivers to turn the very populations they slowly destroyed against the Nex, who might have saved them. This irony had never been lost on Ralston.

"We are friends," Ralston agreed, "but we were more. You were a surrogate for my brother."

"Must we pay respect to dead?" asked Slenth.

"My brother's long dead back on Earth. I meant that I think of you as a brother now." Ralston saw that such a concept meant nothing to Slenth. It never had. Slenth had forty brothers and sisters, all hatched in the same egg-laying season. The Nex shared no familial ties but were strongly bonded to their race. Ralston considered doing a social anthropology paper on this, then discarded the notion as a harmless fantasy. Field archaeology mattered more to him; he had devoted his life to learning what he could of ancient cultures and the process of uncovering the tiny hints that would make those lost races come alive once more, even if only in the pages of some scholarly archaeology journal.

"It's been a long time since we spoke, Slenth. Only a matter of some importance could bring you to Novo Terra. I know how the others treat you. There's no reason to endure that simply to visit me."

Ralston said nothing about skulking around in the dark—armed with the most deadly portable weapons available to modern science.

"Much there is to your work, Ralston. We must never the P'torra allow possession of it."

"You don't want the P'torra to get my work? You've heard of the telepathic projector?"

Slenth rocked his head from side to side indicating Ralston has missed the point.

"It'll be a great benefit. You can train troops even more quickly," said Ralston, remembering the long months he'd spent with Nex psychologists when they hypnotically conditioned him to endure the rigors of interstellar battle. "You can teach your young in a fraction of the time. There is even . . ."

Ralston's words trailed off when he saw Slenth's expression. The burning yellow eyes blazed behind a nictitating membrane. Slenth tensed for battle.

Wordlessly, the Nex drew a small aluminum box from under a cloth covering. A single red light shone. Slenth's taloned finger stroked the side of the box and the light went out. In a gesture he borrowed from his human comrade, Slenth placed that same finger upright across his lips to caution Ralston to silence.

Mouthing the words, Ralston said, "Someone is eavesdropping?"

Slenth nodded vigorously.

Ralston turned to his computer console and began tapping in a sequence of numbers. Over the years, he'd had students barely able to pass his course. He'd exchanged long hours of personal tutoring to get them through his class with minimal passing grades for their expertise in other areas. Mostly,

Ralston had been interested in the University computer system and more than a few of his trouble students had been geniuses when dealing with the network.

One had set up a special account for him that dipped into strange places. Ralston now examined the campus security force's use of the computer system. A parade of numbers dashed across the console. Ralston had to turn to a reference book on the shelf next to his desk and spend several minutes searching until he found matching sequences.

He indicated to Slenth that they should leave. In the hall outside his office, Ralston said, "Security has Chancellor Salazar's permission to spy on me. That was their authorization code. Do you know how they were listening in?"

"Most smaller devices, both sound and looking. They know I and you talked."

"Why didn't you pick up their cameras when we went in?" Ralston had no idea what the small box was that Slenth carried, but he knew it must contain elaborate counterelectronic equipment. The Nex had always been masters at miniaturization and computer technology.

"Microburst reports only sometimes sent. Uncontinual makes difficult to detect."

Ralston thought about the situation. Salazar had violated his rights by authorizing the security force to spy on his office, but this wasn't a matter of any interest to Slenth. It was peripheral to the Nex's purpose for visiting.

"If not the telepathic projector, then what?" asked Ralston.

Slenth cast a quick look at his detector; the red light stayed dark. "The destructor for planets and stars found by you."

"I found nothing of the sort," started Ralston. Then he knew that Slenth meant the chaos device.

The archaeology professor went cold inside. He had wanted to keep the secrets locked within the chaos field away from Salazar and the University because of how they might be misused. He had not thought in broad enough terms, though. He had been too wrapped up in academic politics to remember what the universe did with real weapons. What would the P'torra give for a weapon that could cause a sun to go nova? Or that induced epilepsy in an entire population?

What would the Nex do with that same weapon?

The Nex-P'torra war had petered out and the resolution had been unsatisfactory to both sides, but it had seemed better to cease hostility rather than continue the world-draining interstellar battles. The expense had been great, both in lives and resources. The war had continued, but without casualties that could be tallied and buried. The Nex and the P'torra engaged in trade fights and sabotage that stopped short of sparking another round of open fighting.

Would the Nex use the chaos field against the P'torra home planet?

"Some too fearsome weapons better much to kept away from P'torra," said Slenth, answering Ralston's unspoken question. "That is only Nex goal."

"You're proposing yourselves as caretaker for it?"

Slenth rocked his head in negation. "We need knowledge to prevent P'torra from gaining knowledge. They never against any to use it if Nex hold secret, too."

"A balance of terror is what you're saying. If both sides have the weapon, then neither will use it for fear that the other will retaliate." Ralston watched as Slenth bobbed his head in agreement. "That won't work. It never has."

Ralston closed his eyes and pictured the blackened cinder of Earth. Most of the northern hemisphere had been burned away in short, vicious exchanges. Much of the southern hemisphere and the points just within the arctic circle had been spared. Ralston had been lucky, escaping death through a quirk of fate, but the rest of his family had perished in the first blasts.

"Of Earth history we know well. What else dare we seek to pursue? If P'torra gain use of your device, how many hours go by until against us they use it?"

In that Slenth spoke the truth. The P'torra would never be content to sit on a weapon that potent. If they saw the chance to dominate totally, they would never hesitate.

"It may not even *be* a weapon," protested Ralston. He fell silent when he realized that the race's motive for constructing the chaos field did not enter the argument. No matter what the builders had intended for their device, it could be used as a weapon. Ralston felt more confident with it in Nex hands than in the control of the P'torra, but he wanted neither to use it for destruction.

It brought death and ruin wherever its field touched, but the knowledge to be gained from it was immense. Westcott had spoken of more accurate weather control through predictions based on the equations governing the chaos field. Ralston hoped that epileptic seizures might become predictable using the same mathematics. Hadn't Westcott already successfully predicted which atoms in a radioactive source would decay? What power lay within that? Ralston didn't know, but it couldn't be strictly destructive. The knowledge that threatened destruction could also promise life and a better world.

It had to, or Ralston had no idea what the true purpose of science was.

"This Salazar you as a swimming fish treats you," pointed out Slenth. "P'torra roam at will trouble to cause everywhere. All your peers are scorn filled of you. Give us the knowledge!"

Ralston rubbed his hand over dried lips. He began pacing in the hallway, worrying about the spy devices in his office, Chancellor Salazar, the University and its student unrest, his own career, what unwanted power he controlled. Even the Archbishop agitated against him for his past alliances with the Nex. No matter where Ralston turned in the niche of society he had wanted to call his own, people denounced him. Given enough time, the P'torra would turn the small crowds against him. What had happened to Salazar's secretary would be only the beginning.

Ralston shivered lightly at the thought of being ripped apart by a mob while the P'torra tapped in statistical analyses of the death into his impulse driver.

"I fought alongside the Nex because few other humans would. But I fought as much for them as I did for you. No matter how they behave, I'm not turning my back on them."

"They in the back give you a deadly shot," said Slenth.

"Possibly. Probably. But I can't give you the information you want." Ralston smiled without humor. "I can't give it to the P'torra, either. I simply don't have it. The University would have to fund a considerable expedition to gain such knowledge. Perhaps it's for the best that Salazar denied me funding. Let's leave the chaos device orbiting through space, its secrets untouched."

"Nex will for you give money funds to examine."

The light shiver became a cold shudder of dread. Ralston had gone from having no source of funding to one posing a difficult moral dilemma. The Nex were an honorable race but Ralston didn't want the chaos artifact to be turned into a weapon, even by those he had fought alongside. Better to let it continue through space untouched.

"Many know of this exact orbit chaos machine through space?" asked Slenth.

Ralston stared into the reptile's unblinking yellow eyes. Slenth knew as much about the chaos device as any of those on the expeditions, Ralston saw. Was this the source of the P'torra's veiled warning about choosing companions? The P'torra would want the weapon as much as the Nex. Perhaps more.

Michael Ralston couldn't give it to either.

"Not many," said Ralston. "I've made no attempt to keep it a secret, but the chancellor saw fit to ignore much of my report. Nels Bernssen must have mentioned it in his papers and seminars. Leonore Disa has, also, though her thesis did not specifically refer to it."

"P'torra must not possess secret of randomness," said Slenth. The reptile's talons clicked on the floor to emphasize his concern. "Must *never* learn of its nature."

Ralston struggled to find the words to tell his friend and comrade in arms that the Nex weren't likely to get it from him when a soft click alerted him. He swung around. In the shadows at the far end of the hall he saw a darker figure. A glint of light caught the focusing magnetic muzzle of an energy weapon.

Without thinking, Ralston threw his arms around Slenth and drove forward as hard as he could. The two of them smashed hard into the wall just as a sizzling blue torrent of energy ripped through the space where Ralston had been.

Slenth's reaction time far exceeded that of Ralston. The Nex slithered out of the grip, dropped to the floor, and had his own weapon in action before Ralston could recover his senses. The acrid tang of ozone from the heavy electrical discharges filled the corridor. Ralston stayed low and wiggled toward his office door, pushing it open and getting into the office. The once sturdy-seeming walls of academe would provide no protection against the energy weapon trained on him, but Ralston still felt safer out of sight inside his office.

The computer console blinked slowly, numbers still solemnly marching across the screen. Whoever had put the spy devices in his office now alerted campus security about the brief firefight in progress. Would this save them—or doom them?

"P'torra!" came Slenth's voice. The Nex spit out the name as if it were a curse.

"I thought so. I only caught a glance of him, and he was in the shadows. The focusing muzzle was distinctive, though."

Ralston ventured a quick look around the doorjamb. Slenth had taken cover across the hall behind an uncollected trash receptacle. Down the hall in the shadows came no hint of movement or sound. Ralston waited a few seconds while Slenth's tongue flicked into the air, sampling for the odor of a P'torra.

"Gone," said the Nex. "We must, too. Come and go let us now. Trouble all about."

"Campus security's on its way," said Ralston. "We should wait for them."

"Wait and be ambushed?"

"What do you mean? They won't harm either of us." Ralston's irritation rose to protest such an absurd notion on his friend's part. Salazar and his campus security force might not approve of his archaeology professor and none would like the Nex, but the security force wouldn't harm them.

"What with us will they require?"

"Nothing. We'll have to fill out endless forms but . . ."

"Where to fill such forms out will we go?"

"The main office for security. Across the Quad."

"In wait will P'torra lie to kill us dead. From ambush the fish egg spawn will shoot."

Ralston couldn't answer that, but he did know that no human on the campus force would allow Slenth to keep his energy weapon. Removing it from a dead Nex would be preferable to Slenth simply surrendering it, Ralston knew.

And with all the campus rioting, he had no doubt that the security force would come well armed and ready for a fight. The message flashing on his screen to the University computer would definitely have reported energy weapons discharge— that might incite the campus force to request militia backup.

"Do you want to track down the P'torra?" Ralston asked.

"We must. It kills from back shooting positions. Try to stop P'torra is only course of real logic."

"I don't know how much help I can give you. I don't have a weapon." Ralston remembered his thoughts earlier about attacking the P'torra with his bare hands. The thick blubbery hide would protect the P'torra from any bare-hands attack he might launch.

Ralston blinked when Slenth reached under the harness he wore and pulled free a small energy pack. Ralston took it. The Nex continued to delve into his clothing until he produced the power lead and a small fixed-focus nozzle. Ralston saw that the weapon wasn't much good over ten meters, but that might be enough.

"Just as in old times," said Slenth. The reptile reached out a thin-fingered hand and lightly raked his talons over Ralston's shoulder in a gesture of comradeship.

"Just like old times," Ralston said, feeling dead inside. He'd thought escape into academe relieved him of the old responsibilities, the old duties, the still older fears and doubts.

He'd been wrong.

He and Slenth jogged down the corridor, following the fleeing P'torra's spoor. They'd have only minutes to make the kill before the security force arrived.

FIVE

MICHAEL RALSTON SETTLED the energy weapon in his hand. Old habits returned, as if they had never been broken. He slid the battery pack into his back pocket where it made an uncomfortable lump. Ralston glanced to his right. Slenth glided down the stairs with a silence that Ralston found eerie. They reached the shadowy bottom of the stairs and paused, every sense alert.

Ralston used his vision, which was keener than Slenth's. The reptilian Nex's tongue flicked in and out, sampling, touching the airborne particles for a taste of their prey. In the distance, Ralston heard the whine of sirens as the campus security rushed to the building. For them it had been a long day and one likely to get even longer. Ralston made an impatient gesture to tell Slenth that they'd have to hurry. Once the campus security deployed, they'd have little chance to find and eliminate the P'torra.

Slenth shot toward a door, skidding most of the distance on his belly. Strong back legs propelled him forward, as if this were more a natural mode of movement. For all Ralston knew of the Nex, he was unsure about their preferred posture. They seemed equally suited to slithering on their bellies or walking upright.

"There," said Slenth. His tongue darted in and out. Ralston watched in fascination as both branches of the split tongue vibrated and snapped independently like tiny black leather whips. "P'torra goes without real caution."

"Why'd he try to kill us?" asked Ralston. "He had every-thing going his way." Ralston lengthened his stride to keep pace with Slenth. The Nex covered vast distances without seeming to expend any effort. Ralston found himself panting and in a sweat by the time they reached the crest of a low hill.

"Us? Or you? Many often times the P'torra think in crooked ways. You possess knowledge better dead than given to Nex."

Ralston sucked in a long, deep breath and released it slowly. It had never occurred to him that the P'torra would resort to such overt violence against him. They had always approached the University of Ilium and all those within its system covertly, using their impulse drivers, manipulating and then stepping away to watch. The solitary P'torra now study-ing at the school must have received specific orders from his superiors to dare lose his position by murdering a professor.

Even one like Michael Ralston who was in abject disfavor with the administration.

"Never thought of myself as having such valuable infor-mation."

"Dangerous information," corrected Slenth. "If P'torra their advantage goes away by Nex gaining from you the chaos weapon, they can no more plan sneak attack."

"Sneak attack? Where?"

Slenth looked at him, no hint of his alien nature apparent. He might have been completely human, so poignant and real was the displayed emotion. The membrane covered his yel-low eyes and muted their fire, but the hatred burning there told Ralston that P'torra strategy had not changed since the end of the war. Given the chance, they would launch a sneak attack to wipe out both Nex and humans.

"You need nothing in this to know details of, my good friend," said Slenth.

"They can't find out from me what you know if I fall into their clutches, is that it?" asked Ralston, trying to keep his voice light. He failed. After all this time he again became embroiled in intrigue—and sudden death.

He had almost forgotten their purpose for coming to the top of the quiet, grassy hill. The wavering line of blue-white

energy that sought to rob them of their lives painfully reminded him of the deadly nature of their hunt.

Slenth's strong tail knocked his feet from under him even
as the Nex dived for cover behind a small boulder. The shrub
above his head exploded into flames as the deadly energy
beam shifted and cut through a small arc. The continuous
burn of the weapon had to use up its energy pack quickly.
Ralston tried to decide if the P'torra had more than a few
seconds worth of fire-time left.

He was enough out of practice in such matters not to trust
his own judgment. Long ago during the war, Ralston would
have charged, confident that his enemy had briefly exhausted
his weapon. But only when Slenth shot forward, did Ralston
strike. The Nex still showed great expertise in the ways of
death.

They ran forward a few meters, then split, one going left
and the other right to bracket the P'torra with their fire. The
rustling in the bushes ahead betrayed their enemy's position.
Ralston knew that Slenth's eager tongue had already scented
the P'torra, too.

As one, their energy weapons spat death. Ralston's weapon
guttered and went out after only one long release of fire.
Slenth's continued to surge and seethe for another five seconds.

Ralston and Slenth looked at one another. Ralston nodded.
Even his more feeble sense of smell picked up the charred
flesh odor. They advanced cautiously, both unarmed now
until they could replace their energy packs. Ralston saw that
the caution wasn't needed. A mound of sizzling blubber
stretched a quarter of the way down the hillside. Their beams
had converged directly on target—in the P'torra's face. They
had blown the top quarter of the P'torra apart.

Ralston stood and looked at the gory smear down the softly
grassed hill and felt . . . nothing. It had been this way during
battle. The first time his gorge had risen and he'd thought
he'd be sick. The Nex hypnotic commands had prevented the
horror from impacting too much; getting sick inside a pressure suit helmet could be fatal.

"You remember that first time?" asked Slenth.

Ralston nodded. "We weren't fighting in a poisonous atmosphere this time, but otherwise, no difference." He handed

the useless energy weapon back to Slenth. The Nex slipped it back into the maze of harnesses crisscrossing his slender, scaled body.

"Our really most good fine techniques of mind conditioning hold you yet?"

Ralston found himself unable to speak now. He nodded again, his head feeling as if it would split apart at the seams. The headache started low at the neck, moved up the back of his head, and then burst like some black, evil flower spreading its pollen over his skull.

"Go we must soon," urged Slenth. "Your security forces track carelessly but in this way do finally come."

Ralston turned and went back to the top of the hill. Slenth's appraisal of the University security force's skill proved accurate. A real soldier could have taken them all out with a few quick blasts. But Ralston felt nothing toward them. They assumed duties beyond their training. Even the riots inspired by the P'torra lay beyond most of the security force's coping ability. They patrolled the grassy hills and issued traffic citations and occasionally turned off lights carelessly left on. To deal with this . . ."

"That way," Ralston said, finding his voice.. "We can walk down the hill, circle, and come up behind them. There'll be no indication that we were ever here."

Even as he sketched out their retreat, he studied the ground to be certain that they hadn't left behind damning evidence. The grassy ground didn't take good footprints. Neither of them had dropped incriminating clues. Even with sophisticated forensics equipment, there would be nothing to tie them to the P'torra's death.

They walked away, not hurrying. The mild exercise brought Ralston back to a more normal condition; his battle training once more sank beneath the waves of his mind. But he knew it could resurface anytime he needed it.

"I must not with you be seen," said Slenth. "The questions to be then asked are difficult to answer with properness."

"I'm not sure I'd give you the information about the chaos device, even if I had it," Ralston said suddenly.

"With the Nex you are more safe. With the P'torra . . ."

Slenth pointed back to where they'd killed the humanoid alien.

"Personal safety isn't as important as the possible death of entire planets," said Ralston. "I never thought of myself as an idealist, but maybe I am."

"They can make you die and still the information use. What use of it is this? Allow Nex to furnish expedition. We will not misuse the weapon as would do the P'torra."

"I know, Slenth, I know. But can you promise that the P'torra wouldn't be able to *steal* it from you? Protecting such data might prove impossible."

"Is it the better to let it cast all through space randomly destroying for unknowing any to find and die from?" asked Slenth.

The Nex had a point—and one Ralston had considered. The chaos device had to be neutralized before systems other than the Alpha and Beta died. How many other races had perished over the eons due to its pernicious effects? Ralston didn't know, but if he could only examine its mechanism, determine something of the nature of those beings sending it forth and guess at their purpose, he felt confident that he could dismantle it—or destroy it totally.

"The ways to determine its position are to us also very open," said Slenth. Ralston had no doubt that Westcott or Bernssen or someone else had the same information—better information—concerning the chaos field's current location. One would let the information out, knowingly or otherwise. To stop the information's spread seemed as impossible as returning glue to a tube.

Ralston had to examine the chaos device personally. Soon. And without being obligated to the Nex or the University or anyone else to reveal all the details. If they somehow learned how to control the awesome power generated by the field because of Westcott's work or Bernssen's, at least Ralston would have the small consolation that he had not been the one to unleash it on humans, Nex, or P'torra.

Study it. Destroy it. That seemed the only course open for him. But how?

He started to say something more to Slenth, but the Nex soldier had slipped tracelessly into the night. Ralston wiped

sweat from his forehead as a cool breeze turned it to ice. He
began shaking in reaction to all that had happened. Feet like
lead, he walked slowly to his office, went in, locked the
door, and flopped down hard in his chair.

"To hell with whoever's listening," he said. He lounged
back and hiked his feet to the cluttered desktop. Eyes closed,
he began mentally working through his problems. Ralston
hadn't been in his office five minutes when the door slammed
open and crashed hard into the wall. One book precariously
balanced on a shelf gave up its fight against gravity and fell
noisily.

"The door was locked," Ralston said, eyeing the small,
dark man framed in the doorway. "How'd you open it so
fast?" He'd heard no fumbling outside to alert him to the
intruder.

"Captain Estevez, campus security."

"Captain?" asked Ralston, one eyebrow raised. "Why,
you're just the man I needed to call."

"What?" Estevez was taken off guard.

"Someone's planted spy devices in my office. That's a
direct violation of some law or another, I'm sure. Certainly
it's a violation of my privacy and that of any student who
visits me with a problem, academic or otherwise."

"The Nex. What did you say to him?"

"Now that you've confirmed who planted the devices,
Captain, would you answer why? And who ordered you to do
it? Chancellor Salazar must have better things to do than spy
on me."

"You know that Salazar ordered security to monitor those
most likely to be endangered by the rioters."

"I knew no such thing. Interesting that the chancellor is so
solicitous of my safety after all he's said and done. Perhaps
hell will freeze over yet."

"The Nex. His name is Slenth and he's a high-ranking
officer in their military force. What did you talk about?"

Captain Estevez had a single-minded determination that
Ralston would have appreciated more in a student's devotion
to learning. He studied the man and didn't especially like
what he saw. The razor-tight lips, the narrowed dark eyes, the
set of the body, all spoke of tension and mistrust. Estevez

obviously wished he was elsewhere rather than in the presence of a dangerous campus radical like Ralston.

"Slenth is 'high-ranking'? Good for him. Always was ambitious, even among the Nex."

"You're avoiding the question."

"Captain Estevez of the campus security force gets top marks for an astute observation," said Ralston. He had begun to like this. Estevez could do nothing to him, even if he suspected Ralston's involvement in the P'torra's murder. Estevez would have to call in outside criminal authorities before any arrest could be made. All he wanted was to exercise what little power he had and puff up his self-importance.

Ralston wasn't having any of it.

"You already know everything that went on in this room," said Ralston. "You *are* responsible for the spy devices, after all. Anything I'd add would only be my impression of it."

"You left the room."

"Look around. Do you see any sanitary facilities? No? It might come as a surprise to you, but even professors require such a break now and again."

"The Nex went with you?"

"Strange how biological systems on all planets produce bodily waste that requires evacuation. You might inquire about that with some of the staff in the xenobiology department."

Estevez started to speak, then bit back the words. Barely controlling his anger, he said, "A student was killed tonight."

"I tried to warn Chancellor Salazar about the riots some weeks back. A pity he didn't attach more importance to the events going on outside his office walls."

"He wasn't killed during a riot."

Ralston said nothing.

"He was murdered not two hundred meters from here," Estevez went on.

"In the Quad? I saw nothing. I've had the polarizer on all evening. As you know, I usually enjoy looking out at Bacon's statue, but not tonight. Too much on my mind."

"He wasn't killed on the Quad."

"The only other conclusion I can think of for such questioning, then," said Ralston, "is that he was killed in the faculty restroom and you suspect me."

"Oh, yes, I suspect you. And the Nex." Estevez spat out the last word. "When we have enough evidence, you will not mock us. You will beg for mercy. We know you for what you are, Ralston. You are a murderer and will get no mercy from us!"

"You accuse me of this evening's death? Remember that you're being recorded, Estevez. We have slander laws on Novo Terra. Charge me or apologize."

"I referred to your graduate student. The one you killed on the field expedition."

"De la Cruz died from misadventure. That was the official ruling. I had nothing to do with it." Ralston wanted to add that de la Cruz had died from his own stupidity and avarice but held back.

"We will speak again, Ralston."

"Dr. Ralston to those who spy on me and burst into my office unannounced, Captain." Ralston put as much inflection on the word "captain" as possible to show his contempt.

Estevez spun and stalked off. Ralston waited a few seconds, then crumbled inside. He wasn't cut out for such confrontations. All he wanted to do was archaeology, to dig and think and reconstruct lost cultures and to teach what he knew to eager young students.

When had it all turned to dust?

"We consider this conduct unbecoming to a member of our faculty." The Chancellor of the University of Ilium sat back and folded his hands across his broad chest. Ralston thought Salazar looked like an ancient king back in Earthly Spain's heyday. All Salazar had to say was, "To the dungeons with him!" to make the picture complete.

But the academic world wasn't that blatant. Salazar would find a way to issue the command without it sounding like an intellectual death sentence.

"Are you suggesting that I should have let the students beat your secretary to death? They were well on the way to doing just that when I intervened."

"The four students in question decided not to press assault charges against you, Dr. Ralston."

"Good of them," he said sarcastically. "They aren't going

to press charges against your secretary either, I hope? Especially since he kept throwing himself in front of their fists and feet."

"Your sarcasm only clouds the issue and prejudices this committee against you, Doctor."

"Nothing I could say will prejudice this committee," said Ralston. Under his breath he added, "More than you are now."

"Thank you for the vote of confidence in our objectivity," said Salazar in a neutral tone. "However, we feel that your record of violence is adequate reason to examine your future as professor at this institution."

"Record of violence? You can't be referring to the de la Cruz matter again."

"No, no, nothing of the sort," Salazar said, looking embarrassed. Salazar and Leonid Disa had come to terms over this. Disa had paid off the de la Cruz family in exchange for rights to the telepathic projector Ralston had found. This bartering would not look good on the record for Salazar and he sought to avoid mention of it.

Salazar cleared his throat and hurried on. "I referred to your enlistment with the so-called Nex Planetary Defense Force in that unfortunate war. Further, you have been the target of many of the campus demonstrations because of your past Nex alliances. We are not accusing you of unwonted violence, Dr. Ralston, but you seem to act as a lightning rod for it."

"That's none of my doing."

"But you are still the proximate cause. To allow you to teach the classes already agreed upon for this semester will only incite further unrest among the students."

"I *do* have a contract with the University," Ralston pointed out.

"But no tenure. We can remove you for cause."

"You admitted that I wasn't responsible, Dr. Salazar. Can you dismiss an astronomy professor because the sun comes up and gives everyone sunburn? The University should be committed to a free exchange of ideas, no matter how unpopular."

"We cannot tolerate civil disorder. As you have been

informed by Captain Estevez of our security force, a student was brutally slain last night.''

''Citizen Estevez did allude to it,'' Ralston said cautiously. The feeling he got from the others on the Committee on Academics and Freedom was one of increasing uneasiness. They were not happy with the notion of firing a professor innocent of anything but irritating the chancellor. But they were also astute political animals seeking their own survival. To cross Salazar in this matter would put them next on his list. One or two would be up for tenure hearing soon, Ralston knew. A wrong vote might jeopardize their position.

Better to oust a rebel like Michael Ralston than to lose their own positions. Ralston read this clearly on several faces.

But the uneasiness remained—and grew. All thought the same thing: If Salazar did this to Ralston, he could do it to any of them. For any reason.

''Dr. Salazar,'' spoke up a man at the far end of the long table. ''My esteemed colleague has a point about his culpability in this distasteful unrest among some of our more immature students.'' Ralston almost choked when he followed the line of Velasquez's thinking. The man had successfully plundered Proteus of several technological gadgets and had consolidated his position. To him Ralston presented no challenge, but one never knew.

Ralston knew what Velasquez would propose as clearly as if he could read the other archaeologist's mind.

''However,'' Jaime Velasquez went on smoothly, ''this unrest is not to be lightly dismissed. The death of our only P'torra student points this out.''

''What are you saying, Dr. Velasquez?'' asked Salazar, irritated at having his line of thought interrupted.

''Dr. Ralston is a valued and capable member of the University community and it would be ridiculous to penalize him for events beyond his control. We can use his talents, both in the field and in the classroom.'' Jaime Velasquez smiled winningly. ''However, his presence only causes more unrest. Perhaps he should consider taking a year's sabbatical. It has been some time since he sampled other teaching methods in other institutions. Many schools on other planets would welcome him for his ability.''

"An excellent idea, Dr. Velasquez," said Salazar. The quick, nervous nods up and down the table showed that the committee favored this easy way out.

"But, Chancellor!" protested Ralston. "I'd need several months to arrange everything. I've not checked at other schools for available positions."

"I'm placing you on immediate sabbatical, Dr. Ralston. I realize that this might constitute a vacation without pay for you until you can find another university position, but it is necessary. Ilium's budget has come under fire from the Regents and we simply cannot afford the luxury of a non-teaching professor on our payroll. I'm sure a man of your academic caliber and superior standing will readily find another school for your sabbatical."

Salazar raised and dropped his small gavel, signifying the matter had been closed, that justice had been served, and embarrassment for the University again avoided. Ralston started to protest, to demand a hearing of the full faculty, then turned and left without speaking. They hadn't had the courage to fire him outright, but they had gotten rid of him just as surely as if they had.

Damn Salazar! Damn them all!

Michael Ralston had no idea what he was going to do. Accepting Slenth's offer still carried the seeds of universal destruction with it, yet he had no other way of reaching the chaos device without some source of financing now that the school's field research funds were totally closed to him.

What was he to do? Ralston walked aimlessly, in a vain attempt to find an answer.

SIX

MICHAEL RALSTON DROPPED the last of his archaic reference books into a box, then reached over and began working on his computer console—his former console, he mentally corrected. Within a few minutes, he had permanently locked his records onto the University files. If he ever returned, he'd be able to pick up the work where he had left it. But the most important component of his work wasn't inside any computer data bank but in his head.

He sighed and looked around the tiny cubicle that had been his sanctuary for the past three years. He knew it'd be for the last time. No other university would take him on sabbatical on such short notice. No off-planet school would consider a request now, unless his luck improved and he managed to coordinate well with a starting time slightly different from those on Novo Terra.

Offhand, Michael Ralston didn't know of any he'd care to teach at. And with no funds available, he wouldn't be able to simply do research. His field work was expensive. Even old proton magnetometers cost a young fortune.

"Michael?" came a familiar voice. He looked up to see a brown-haired, somewhat plain woman in the door. Ralston noted that Leonore Disa was about the same height as the captain of University security; their heads cast a shadow at about the same point on the door.

"You can either come in and watch me finish packing, or you can help me. Take your pick."

"Always the latter," she said, smiling. He'd seldom seen her happier. But then, Leonore had good reason to be happy. Finishing off her doctorate had been a milestone in her life. Soon, she and Nels Bernssen would be married. Another happy event.

"You're the only one who hasn't come by to gloat. Velasquez is particularly vicious."

"I'd heard it was his idea to send you off to limbo. What'd you ever do to him?"

"Rivalry over Proteus. He knew that dig should have been mine. And I'm sure he's gone over my data from Alpha. *That's* the real find, and he knows it. This is his way of increasing the importance of his work and decimating mine."

Leonore perched on the edge of his desk, silently noting the dull computer screen and the filled boxes. She swung her leg back and forth in a nervous pattern that made Ralston want to reach down and grab it to still the pendulum motion.

"Nels is finishing a seminar," she said. "He can't work hard enough to fight off the recruiters." Leonore wrinkled her pug nose and made a wry face. "I really *don't* like the one from the University of New Salamanca. She's pretty and she knows it."

"Trying to lure him away using sex, eh?"

"Worse than that. She knows her physics better than any of the others going after Nels. *That's* the part that worries me."

Ralston had to laugh. "Makes me consider changing fields. Think she'd like to recruit a former archaeologist?"

"Why former?" asked Leonore. "That is, unless you just want to hang around campus."

"You've heard of the offers, then?" he asked. "I can't get caught between the Nex and the P'torra over the chaos field. I just can't. I'd prefer it in Nex hands, but trusting them—even Slenth—isn't easy. You know what Lord Acton said."

" 'Power corrupts, absolute power corrupts absolutely,' " Leonore answered.

Ralston smiled. His best students knew more than the narrow field of archaeology. But then the best in any field always knew more than just their subject. That was part of what made them so special.

"Getting back to what you were saying, Michael, no, I hadn't heard about the Nex offering you anything. I suspect Daddy would make an offer, but he's been off planet for a month now and can't know anything about this."

Ralston perked up. He looked squarely at his former student. "There's another offer?"

"Nels is turning down all the offers to speak. And he's already turned down five teaching positions, one of them an endowed chair with the promise of tenure after one year. He's put together a half-dozen grants that'll fund a really good expedition this time."

"But it'll be his expedition," said Ralston, his hope fading. What an astrophysicist would want from the chaos device differed mightily from what an archaeologist needed.

"Of course it will, mostly."

"Mostly? What part won't?"

"Mine. I got a pair of unlimited-scope research grants, no restrictions, no reports required, nothing but field study. *I* want to study the device as badly as you do, Michael. Come with us. Please. We need your expertise."

"The only reason you didn't hear a sonic boom as I accept and race to the shuttle launcher is that I'm weighed down with all these books. Help me get them home, then let's sign some papers."

"You don't mind working for me, rather than the other way around? That's the way it'll have to be."

Ralston swallowed his pride. He wanted all his students to do well on their own. Leonore Disa had certainly succeeded beyond his expectations for a new Ph.D. But to work under such a recently former student might be seen as degrading.

He didn't care. He'd be in space and on the track of that damned elusive chaos field!

"I'll scrub the decks to study the device," he said, meaning every word of it.

"No contracts, then. Your word is good enough." Leonore thrust out her hand. Ralston engulfed the small hand in his larger one and shook vigorously.

He almost glowed from the anticipation of again being in space on the chaos device's trail as he carried his boxes out and loaded them onto a truck. Ralston didn't even notice the watchful eyes of Captain Estevez on him as he worked.

He was going back to space to unlock the most perplexing, the most dangerous, the most significant puzzle of a lifetime!

"It hardly seems enough," Ralston said, studying the pile of their equipment. For every small box he and Leonore had been allowed, Nels Bernssen and his crew of fourteen astrophysicists had a score of large ones. "But it is his expedition. We're going to have to discuss what it is he wants when we find the device, and how to best get it without interfering with our work."

"I want to check out the markings," said Leonore. "The Betan reported curious hieroglyphic characters that sounded similar to those on a couple of other planets. We might be dealing with a race that has visited other worlds, then left messages."

Ralston shook his head. It was a pity only one creature had seen the chaos device passing through the Beta system. The Betan had not been a reliable observer. By the creature's own admission, it was regarded as insane by its peers. Ralston couldn't pass judgments like that, but he knew that a creature living under ten atmospheres of ammonia and methane pressure didn't have the same perceptions of the universe that warm-blooded mammals did.

Ralston looked over the shuttle launch area. Here and there concrete depressions dotted the tarmac, immensely powerful pulsed lasers at the bottom of the pits. The stubby shuttles would be launched by the action of the laser against splash plates until orbit, then tiny steering jets would move the shuttle to their starship. Ralston had gone this route many times, but still a sense of eagerness lingered and kept him on edge. Out among the stars lay the traces of cultures long dead. He would put all the pieces together and discover what had been lost for eons. The anticipation of actually seeing the chaos device made him forget all that had gone on at the University.

Almost.

"Ready to do science?" came Nels Bernssen's deep voice. Ralston looked over his shoulder. Nels hadn't been speaking to him but to Leonore. A pang caught at Ralston's throat. The expedition leader spoke to the secondary leader—and it wasn't him. It was his former student. Former, recent student.

Michael Ralston pushed such feelings away with some difficulty and went to where Bernssen checked off the masses of Leonore's equipment on a manifest.

"Looks like you made the limit. Even came in a microgram or two under."

"Does that mean we can pack something else?" asked Ralston.

Bernssen laughed at this. "Hell no, it means I don't have to throw out something I might need when we get there. I wish we were all traveling as light as Westcott." He gestured in the mathematician's direction. Westcott sat silently on a plastic crate, eyes glazed and his head-mounted IR sensor covered by a knit hood. It made him appear even less human than he was.

Leonore saw Ralston eyeing the sensor covering and said, "I knitted it for him. I couldn't stand staring at the hardware gleaming on the top of his head. It still gives me the cold shudders."

"I know what you mean," said Ralston.

"Has Westcott shown you the plots for his equations?" asked Bernssen. "The more I think about the color scheme the more I like it. I think there might be other applications for the technique."

"The colors are lovely," said Ralston, not caring that much about mathematical processes. He wanted to be aboard the shuttle and lifting for orbit, away from Novo Terra and the University. Only then could they star out and find the alien chaos device.

Bernssen slapped Ralston on the shoulder and said, "We'll be on our way soon. Try to relax. Enjoy the trip, Michael. Let Leonore do the work." Nels smiled broadly. "After all, it is her first expedition where she's in charge of worrying."

Nels had meant the comment to be light and reassuring. Ralston couldn't take it that way. He flashed a fake smile and let Bernssen get on with the final loading and stowing of their equipment. Reluctantly, Ralston went and sat beside Westcott. The mathematician acknowledged his presence with a quick dart of his eyes. Other than this small movement, the man didn't stir.

"The basins of attraction are diminished in the latest plot," said Westcott.

"What?" Taken aback, Ralston turned and stared at the mathematician. He had no idea what he meant.

"In my plot. The dark areas are always stable and tend toward the strange attractors, points that are either fixed or periodic."

"So?"

"The colored areas of the graph are unstable." Westcott's eyes seemed to focus on his color plots rather than anything at the shuttle site. "The colors are expanding, taking over all the graph. The instability is increasing."

"What were you plotting?" Ralston asked, suddenly worried at Westcott's tone.

"The equation governing the device itself. I believe I've found the underlying equation that creates the field. I did a time progression on it. And it's decaying. It's becoming more chaotic."

"And less predictable?"

"It was never predictable, not in the sense you mean. But my mathematics is unable to deal with it."

"What does this mean?" asked Ralston. "Put it in words I can understand."

"The field is intensifying and creating more and more chaos as it travels. It might not last another year."

"But you can't be sure of that, can you? This is all speculation. You can't know." Cold panic clutched at Ralston's throat. The chaos device had triggered novas that destroyed his greatest finds. It couldn't be so unstable that it'd self-destruct before he had a chance to determine its planet of origin and something about its builders. It just couldn't do that to him! Not after all he'd been through.

"No, I'm not sure. But the mathematics is precise enough to describe the general trend of the equations. How fast the chaotic effect spreads, when and if it become self-destructive, those I can't say with any certainty."

Ralston relaxed.

"It might not be a year. It might be a month." Westcott spoke with such confidence that Ralston wilted.

"The only problem I see," Westcott went on, "is in my not being able to record directly the effects on the appropriate tensors surrounding it. Can't study what's no longer there."

Westcott rubbed his chin slowly. "In this case, it might be possible. The equations go to infinity at different speeds. The colors show that."

Westcott hopped off the crate and wandered away, muttering to himself. Ralston wanted to call out and warn him not to blunder into a laser pit, then stopped. It might be better if the mathematician did something like that. He had no right depressing Ralston even more by telling him the chaos device was unstable and would soon blow up or fall apart or whatever its particular course of destruction was.

"Launch in one hour!" called out Nels Bernssen. "Get aboard and let's button up. I want to get to orbit and star out of here as soon as possible."

Ralston went toward the squat shuttle, no longer excited about the prospects ahead. The future would repeat the past. His greatest achievement would be ripped away by chaos and he'd be left with nothing. Nothing at all.

Ralston lay in the acceleration couch staring at a gray carbon composite bulkhead. He imagined he could almost see the individual whiskers that made the light plate so strong. He began to twitch and stir against the web harness, then shucked off the straps and sat up to look around.

On the other side of the small compartment Westcott lay with his eyes closed. He might have been sleeping or lost in his mathematical fantasy world. Ralston didn't know and wasn't going to disturb him to find out. His restlessness increased when he failed to hear the usual whine of servomotors getting the shuttle ready to launch. If anything, the ship was too quiet.

It sat as if deserted.

Ralston swung out of the couch and made his way to the tube running the length of the shuttle. Upward lay the cockpit where the pilot balanced the ship on the vicious end of the laser. Ralston craned around but saw no one above. He deftly spun about and caught the rungs in the tube and descended a level. Leonore Disa slept quietly in one couch. Bernssen's was empty beside hers.

Ralston frowned. Going lower he found the rest of the expedition either dozing or idly chatting, most of them bored

and wishing to get into space. Ralston talked with the two
nearest the tube but they had no idea what the delay was.

Coldness formed in Ralston's guts. In earlier, happier days
he would have shrugged it off and decided that something
minor held them back, something of no real importance. Now
he feared the worst. He dropped down the long access tube
and landed in a crouch just inside the airlock. Both doors
stood open, indicating that pressurization for launch hadn't
even begun.

He crept forward and almost fearfully looked out. Nels
Bernssen and the shuttle pilot stood at the edge of the launch
pit arguing with three men. Ralston frowned. Those three
looked familiar but he couldn't place them.

When Captain Estevez came up and joined the group, he
recognized them as campus security.

Ralston was too far away to hear over the clanking and
pounding and electrical crackling that came from the field,
but their stance gave him a good idea what was going on.
Another man came up and spoke quickly with Estevez, then
turned and spoke to Bernssen. The disgusted expression on
the newcomer's face and the way he dismissed Estevez told
of authority exceeding any mere campus policeman.

Ralston held back from descending to ground level and
seeing what the officers wanted. He could guess. Estevez had
followed him for days after their confrontation, no doubt
looking for some minor violation. When Ralston had been
sent packing from the University, that should have ended
Estevez's interest.

It hadn't.

The peace warden turned and pointed toward the open
airlock. Ralston wasn't able to slip back inside quickly enough.
Over the noise on the field he heard a bull-throated yell, "Get
down here, Ralston. Now!"

Bernssen and the pilot huddled together, then Bernssen
motioned for Ralston to come down. Whatever happened,
Bernssen was his friend, but the physicist wasn't going to
jeopardize the expedition for that friendship. To him, finding
the chaos device was more important than any single member
of the team.

Perhaps even more important than Leonore Disa, though

Ralston wouldn't want to go that far in judging Bernssen's devotion to his work. But he could definitely say that Nels would throw him to the dogs rather than delay much longer.

Ralston saw no reason to not obey. He went down the ladder slowly, his mind racing. Estevez and the peace warden could want any number of things from him, but the one that lodged firmly in his head was the death of the P'torra. That was the only capital crime he'd committed that would be worth the time of so many enforcement officers.

After all, Salazar had successfully rid himself of a problem by sending Ralston on an enforced year-long sabbatical. He had no reason to detain him.

"Dr. Ralston?" said the man with Estevez. "Warden Kolkoff, assigned to investigate the student's death."

"They're going to hold up launch until they talk with you," cut in Bernssen. "Make it quick. We have a launch window to meet or we have to lay over an extra day." Bernssen referred to the starship in orbit. Departures and arrivals were carefully regulated. It might even be necessary to cancel the departure from orbit and wait for another week or more.

Ralston felt as if time crushed down around him. He couldn't get Westcott's comments out of his mind. The chaos device had reached a point of instability where it might destroy itself at any time. After hundreds of thousands, perhaps millions, of years, it had chosen this particular year to chaotically fall apart.

Not for the first time, Ralston wanted to scream, "It's not fair!"

"I've already told Estevez all I know about the death. A P'torra, wasn't it? I think I saw that on the news."

"That's what makes the matter so delicate," said Kolkoff. "The P'torra ambassador is understandably upset. That makes my superiors upset and, well . . ." The peace warden spread his hands and tried to smile winningly. He failed.

"I understand all that," said Ralston. "I don't understand why you're delaying us."

"We feel you know more about the P'torra's death than you told Captain Estevez. A lot more." Kolkoff ran a finger under his nose, as if wiping away sweat or trying to keep from sneezing. "I just looked over his preliminary report and, well, sir, I must agree. You should come with us for questioning."

"Nels!" Ralston looked to the tall blond. Ralston saw the pale eyes harden. Quick calculations went through both his and the pilot's mind. Ralston preferred those that Nels worked on. If they reached orbit in time to transfer, they could star out before the authorities on planet stopped them.

Even as the thought flashed across Nels' mind, it vanished. A simple radio message to starship control would stop them.

Nels Bernssen wouldn't halt his expedition for Ralston. Never. Help if he could, yes, but not stop the expedition. Too much rode on the man's shoulders for that.

"Nels," Ralston said quickly, "if we got up without being stopped, could we make it out of orbit within a few hours?"

"Within an hour," spoke up the pilot. "We've been delayed enough. We're damn close to the launch time. I'd barely have time to unload the equipment and secure it in the starship's hold before you'd be on your way. I need to get free of the ship's drive field before it shifts. That means another hour. You'd need a minimum of three hours after we hit orbit, just to be sure."

"Dr. Ralston, this isn't a smart course of action on your part," said Kolkoff. "Resisting only makes it appear that you *do* know more than you've said. Perhaps you're involved in a more significant way."

Peace Warden Kolkoff stepped back and reached into a pocket. Although he didn't reveal what lay inside, Ralston guessed it was a stun weapon and it was aimed directly at him. Any attempt to resist and he'd end up flopping about on the ground in extreme pain, his nervous system jumbled for hours.

Ralston, Kolkoff, Estevez, and the three campus security men with him turned to go back to a low shed where their aircars were parked when the archaeology professor saw something that returned hope.

Over his shoulder, he called, "I'll be up in a minute, Nels. Get everything ready, but don't close up till the last possible instant."

"Dr. Ralston," said Kolkoff in a tired voice. "The only place you're going is—"

Ralston dropped forward, catching himself on his hands. His right foot swung out and back in a short, vicious arc that caught Kolkoff behind the knee. The peace warden yelped and lost his balance, falling backward. As Estevez and the others turned, an energy beam crackled just above their heads.

They, too, dropped to the ground.

"Run into your ship at the launch," came Slenth's command. "These five are not to move about too soon until you can go."

"I'll need at least three hours, maybe more."

"They will my company enjoy for this and even more so time," said the Nex. "All are sane and not wanting to be fried in the energetic beam of my weapon."

"Thanks. Thank you." Ralston clapped Slenth on the Nex's slender shoulder, then turned and ran for the ladder.

"You won't get away with this!" called Kolkoff.

Ralston saved his breath for running. He jumped and caught the fifth rung up and climbed like his distant ancestors must have when they swung in the trees. Ralston somersaulted through the airlock and cycled it shut.

"Who was that?" asked Bernssen. "Never mind. I recognized him as a Nex. I don't think I want to know any more about what you're involved in."

"We've got four hours. Can we really get our equipment transferred and star in that time?"

"We'll have to, won't we?" said Bernssen.

Ralston barely made it to his acceleration couch before the pulsed laser fired and slammed them up into the sky and toward the waiting starship.

SEVEN

RALSTON JERKED AND sent himself spinning away into an elastic protector mounted on the starship bulkhead when Nels
Bernssen called out, "We're ready to go!"

The others gathered in the starship's main lounge spun
around to anchor themselves down for the gentle rocket shove
that would take them out of orbit around Novo Terra and send
them flying faster than light toward the Beta system.

"Any contact from planetside?" Ralston asked anxiously.
Bernssen's head hardly moved as he shook it. Ralston didn't
know whether to relax now and assume all was well or to
keep worrying. Slenth might even confess to the murder to
free Ralston of suspicion. The Nex might enjoy some form of
diplomatic immunity; Ralston didn't know. Whatever happened with Kolkoff and Estevez, once the stardrive engaged,
they were beyond the reach of any planetary authority.

Ralston closed his eyes and hung weightlessly. Although it
might not be true, after his escape from Kolkoff, he had to
reckon himself a fugitive from justice. The entire Novo Terra
peace staff would be seeking him for murdering the P'torra.
At best, he would be considered Slenth's accessory, a crime
carrying only slightly less penalty than the actual commission
of the murder itself.

But in his own mind, Ralston had killed the P'torra. His
finger twitched, the same finger that had curled around
the energy weapon's trigger and sent the blast of energy
blazing out to cinder the alien. The P'torra wasn't the first he

71

had killed in such a fashion. Michael Ralston could only hope
that this one would be the last. He didn't like the gut-chilling
sensation of taking another being's life, even a P'torra's.

A fugitive. He ran like a coward. All that Salazar had said
about him would be believed without question now. Michael
Ralston, former University of Ilium professor, had murdered
a student and then fled with the aid of his accomplice, the
dastardly Nex mercenary and murderer, Slenth.

He *had* killed the P'torra, but it had been in self-defense,
although a jury would find this difficult to believe. He and
Slenth had hunted the blubbery alien creature down and ambushed him. It wouldn't matter that the P'torra had attacked
first. They had followed and killed him. That was the hinge
point of the law. His and Slenth's lives were no longer in
danger and yet they'd chosen to find the P'torra and kill, kill,
kill.

Ralston's head felt as if it would explode from the tension.
He jumped when hands touched the back of his neck.

"Relax," Leonore Disa said softly. "You're too tense.
When we star, you're going to be turned inside out."

"You know what happened planetside?"

"Nels told me. I don't for an instant believe you had
anything to do with the P'torra's death."

"But you'd believe Slenth responsible."

Leonore frowned, not understanding. "You mean the Nex
who took the peace warden prisoner?"

"That's Commander Slenth, of the Nex Planetary Defense
Force. The best friend any soldier in the field can have."

Leonore's fingers worked at the tight knots on his shoulders. Ralston couldn't keep from wincing. He'd reacted more
strongly to his problems than he'd thought; even with Leonore's
expert kneading, the muscles refused to relax.

She said nothing for a few minutes, then pushed back.
Ralston half turned and hung suspended so that he could
look into her brown eyes. What he read there did not surprise
him.

"Yes," he said, knowing that the truth would be better
than a lie, even if it did change the way she thought of him.
"Slenth and I did kill the P'torra. It was in self-defense, but

no human jury would believe that. They'd be too quick to condemn a Nex.'' Ralston laughed bitterly. ''And if Salazar could add a vexing problem professor to the murderer's indictment, he'd do it.''

''You're selling yourself short, Michael,'' she said. ''I don't pretend to approve of killing the P'torra, but if you say it was self-defense, it was. I just wish you'd have told the authorities. They'd not condemn you without examining the evidence.''

''There wasn't much evidence left,'' he said. ''Slenth and I are good with energy pistols.''

''There's the signal,'' Leonore said. ''We're ready to blast out of orbit.''

Only then did Ralston begin to let the tension drain from him. Once free of Novo Terra's gravity well, return wouldn't be easy. At a few AU's, the star shift would occur and they'd be past any planetary control.

The rockets gently forced him into the restraining pad. The red indicator light flashed faster and faster until it became a steady glow. At one-tenth of a gee, the ship accelerated from its parking orbit. Two midcourse corrections later, their heavy gyroscope spun to hold their axis steady and the pilot lined them up precisely for the light years-distant Beta system.

A green light began flashing to indicate the approaching shift. When it went solid green, Ralston gasped involuntarily, his heart stopping, his lungs freezing, and the universe turning into a maelstrom of swirling colors more intense than anything Westcott had plotted using his chaos equations.

For an infinite time, Ralston swam through the colors, tasting them, letting them coolly caress his cheeks, his eyelids, the inside of his skin. Only slowly did the colors fade and his senses return to normal.

Many of the others had recovered from the drive's unpredictable side effects but he had asked and no one else experienced the disorienting sensory shifts. A few times Ralston experienced no sensory confusion. But the last three or four shifts had been particularly devastating to his equilibrum.

''You look pale. Are you all right?'' Bernssen asked anxiously. The big blond drifted nearby, one long arm curled around Leonore's slender waist.

"I . . . I'm fine," answered Ralston. "The shifts are getting harder for me."

"Ever since you used the telepathic projector on Beta 5," said Leonore. "You touched on the chaos-induced epilepsy of the Alphans then."

"I did?" Ralston still felt disoriented, confused. He remembered nothing about that.

"You did," Leonore said, concern for Ralston mounting. "You went into a seizure. It wasn't a grand mal seizure, but it was strong enough to frighten me. You became the Alphan scientist and you endured what he had—an epileptic seizure."

"A chaotic event," cut in Westcott. The mathematician drifted by, his infrared sensor unit blinking. Across the large lounge he had mounted a receiver onto a linking unit that put him into contact with the ship's main computer. Once again, Westcott was whole.

"Call it what you want," Leonore said, "but it might have permanently affected him." Leonore rotated and faced Ralston again. "You did get a complete physical when you got back to the University?"

"The doctor couldn't find anything wrong. Gave me an unconditional pass. But how could he check for shift-related problems without putting me through the dimensional changes?"

"Doesn't matter," said Westcott in his smug tone. "A chaotic event isn't going to be obvious. The residual effects might linger for years. Perhaps forever."

"I don't remember this seizure," Ralston said.

"Part of it." Westcott nodded sagely, a smirk on his lips. "You might have patches of memory loss similar to a stroke. Pinpoint losses you'd never notice unless a complete brain map has been made and a comparison can be done."

"I've never had it done," said Ralston. "There didn't seem to be any reason."

"He won't suddenly forget or have another seizure, will he?" Leonore put Ralston's fears into words.

"We're dealing with randomness induced mathematically. It is wonderful, isn't it?" gloated Westcott. "We have the chance to observe the results of chaos on otherwise orderly systems."

"The system you're talking about is *me*!" Ralston shouted. Several others in the lounge turned to see what caused the commotion. The lowered air pressure saved Ralston from complete embarrassment. Only those closest heard his outburst. The others continued their private conversations undisturbed.

"How can I be sure I'm not carrying the seeds of chaos within me?" he asked in a more controlled tone.

"There's no way to know," said Westcott. "I suspect you are. I suspect all who were on either Alpha 3 or Beta 5 and were touched by the residual effects of the field are tainted. Yes, tainted is a good way of putting it. Very good. Nothing major wrong with us, but small parts no longer function properly."

"You mean my liver might give out because of the chaos field?" asked Leonore.

"I doubt that, unless we come into direct contact with the fully functioning field. However, your hormone balance might be subtly different. Or a gene might have toggled. Probably nothing significant is wrong inside your head. Possibly you have triggered an oncogene and cancer is even now beginning to devour your body. Who can say? It's all random, after all."

"You're able to determine mathematically what's going on!" cried Ralston, still upset.

"Only in special cases. The radioactive decay calculation is a phenomenal breakthrough. But to predict, say, weather patterns? Not yet. My computations need more sophistication, more elegance. These are nonlinear differential equations we're dealing with. The slightest parameter change results in a wild fluctuation. I showed you the mapping I did."

"The colored plots?"

"The black is stable, the red is most unstable, the most chaotic. The greens and blues show a slower trending toward the unstable. This is how I determined that the chaos field generating device is quickly becoming unstable. It has acted upon itself long enough to begin to introduce increasing random behavior."

Ralston couldn't bring himself to carry on with the conversation. He kicked against an elastic band and began slowly drifting into the center of the chamber. Already most of Bernssen's colleagues had left, gone to attend to their various duties. Boredom destroyed more expeditions than any danger among the stars and Bernssen wanted his researchers busy from the first minutes of the trip.

Ralston felt strong fingers circle his ankle. Nels Bernssen pulled alongside until the two of them floated eye to eye. By speaking quietly, they were effectively isolated from the few who remained.

"Are you all right, Michael? You're looking worse every time I see you."

"I'm fine. Really."

"You don't sound it. And that business back on Novo Terra is going to be difficult to sort out when you return. You know that, I hope."

"I know." Bleakness filled Ralston. Westcott said the chaos device fell apart daily and might vanish totally before they tracked it down and a murder charge hung over his head like the Sword of Damocles. He had no job and had been allowed to accompany this expedition only through Leonore's influence with Bernssen.

"I'm going to need you, Michael. A great deal, when we find the chaos device. You'll have to do all the preliminary work."

"What?" This brought Ralston back. "I thought all you wanted to do was measure the physical fields around it."

"Westcott says the device might be more conceptual than physical. Whatever that means, we're going to need someone to decipher the motives of the race constructing it. If my crew can tear it apart and find out how it works, they will. But there might not be much to rip into. We'll need all the information we can get on the race building it, what they looked like, how they thought, how their civilization functioned. We'll need it all to even begin to understand."

"Leonore's idea about the markings might not be far off, but I've got a few other notions of my own. We can . . . ."

"Good," said Bernssen, smiling broadly. "That's your area, not mine. You don't need to know about proton-proton cycles or any of the rest of the subatomic particle jungle. And you need only give me the results of your work. A deal?''

"Done!"

Bernssen waved to Leonore, then kicked off and drifted to join her. Ralston wasn't sorry to see the physicist go. He wanted a little time alone to think this through. Perhaps he wasn't as useless as he'd thought. A good picture of the society building the chaos device *would* help Bernssen. Ralston hadn't thought that the physicist recognized that. But he did and Ralston wanted to do everything possible to help.

Ralston left the lounge and made his way down the shaft running the length of the starship. When he came to the storage area, he found himself waiting in line to get to his equipment crates. A half dozen of Bernssen's expedition wanted access to their equipment, too, to calibrate, to study, to prepare.

"Give me a hand, will you?" asked one earnest young man. He sweated as he wrestled with a heavy crate.

"You'll never get it out that way. Inertia," Ralston reminded the physicist. The idea that he, as a seasoned space hand, could tell the youngster about his own field bolstered his confidence even more. Together, they fastened down a few crates and used a block and tackle arrangement to gently pull the needed equipment crate free. Storage had been done haphazardly due to the lack of time before leaving Novo Terra orbit. Ralston made a mental note to tell the pilot that they should rearrange everything before shifting back into normal space. It wouldn't help the handling of the starship but it would protect valuable equipment from possible damage.

"Thanks," the man said, once they'd retrieved the desired instruments. "Calibration's going to take me a couple weeks. Then I have to set up in the lounge or on these walls." He looked around, sizing up potential mounting spots. "Dr. Bernssen wants everything ready to go the instant we shift into the Beta system."

"First expedition?" Ralston asked. He knew the answer before the man answered.

"That it is. I read about Dr. Bernssen and his successes with predicting the nova conditions and knew I had to be on his next trip. I just *had* to. This is where science is being done and I want to be a part of it.'' The young man looked at Ralston more carefully, recognition slowly dawning on him.

"You're one of the grave robbers, aren't you?'' The man clamped his mouth shut quickly when he realized he must have insulted Ralston.

"I've been called worse."

"Sorry. We were told to keep the jokes to a minimum since Dr. Bernssen's marrying one of you."

"You make us sound like aliens. We're just plain folks who enjoy digging around in lost garbage to find out why it was discarded, who did it, and something about why it should be left."

"Sounds dirty to me. I prefer something clean. I do spectrographic work in solar coronas, specializing in iron sublimations."

Ralston had no idea what the young man meant.

"Good luck," said Ralston, beginning his hunt through the piles for his own crates. "Hope all your lines come out nice and sharp."

"Thanks. And thanks for helping me. No matter what the others say, you're all right." He thrust out his hand and said, "My name's McGhee. Glad to meet you, Dr. Ralston."

Ralston laughed at this. He knew the physicists under Bernssen might gossip a little, but they had no time to discuss the likes of an archaeologist. They'd be more inclined to talk about Leonore and Nels. For the first time since boarding the research ship, Ralston felt a part of this expedition, accepted by Nels and Leonore and now by one junior member.

He searched until he found their small cache. Leonore Disa had arranged for a pair of "supervisors," sophisticated controllers that would keep track simultaneously of more than a hundred different automated probes. If time proved to be of the essence—and Ralston knew it would because of the chaotic effects induced into electronic circuitry by the field— they might have only a few seconds before everything failed. All needed data had to be gathered in those precious instants.

His equipment crates had been better designed than those used by the physicists. Side panels snapped off to allow easy entry without moving the crate from its stack. Ralston burrowed into one to find the first set of probes. He needed to calibrate their spectral responses to view everything from hard x-ray through soft infrared. This covered any possible visual input.

Ralston peered up from his work when he heard loud clanging. To his surprise he saw the pilot working hard to pull off an access hatch to the ship's electronics.

"Need help?" he called out. Pilots were notorious loners, having as little to do with their passengers as possible. Ralston didn't want to irritate the man a single hour into a journey of over six weeks.

"Can use it," the pilot grunted. "Damn ship's falling apart already."

"What's wrong?" Ralston knew pilots were as close to perfectionists as anyone in the galaxy. Few starships failed to return because of malfunction.

"Not much," the pilot grumbled. He was a smallish man with Leonore Disa's coloration. His light brown hair flew in a wild disarray that made Ralston wonder if the man had already touched a live circuit and electrocuted himself. Powerful hands with thick, short fingers pried open the hinged hatch and revealed a mind-numbing array of block circuits and other electronic paraphenalia. Ralston had no idea what this panel controlled.

"Here, put your finger here. Press hard. Harder, dammit," the pilot snapped. Ralston did as he was told. The block circuit he shoved against sank a few centimeters, then began to heat.

"What's supposed to happen?"

"Nothing. That's what's wrong. St. Christopher, why does this happen to me? I ask you, why?" The man swung around to brace his feet against the bulkhead above Ralston, then began inputing a string of numbers into the control console.

"It's getting hotter," Ralston said. "And I think it's sinking even farther into the board."

"Don't let go. Whatever you do, don't let go!" The panic in the pilot's voice worried Ralston.

"This controls our shift mechanism, doesn't it?"

"Damn right it does. Lose this baby and we're dead in space. Noticed that the redundant circuits had blown. All three of them. God in space, why isn't this working?"

Ralston yelped in pain when the block circuit heated up to the point where he couldn't bear it. Reflexively, he jerked his hand away, allowing the block to rise back from its depression.

Instantly, alarm bells throughout the ship began their strident message of disaster. The lights in the cargo hold dimmed and Ralston fought to see even the pilot less than a meter distant.

But the pilot's words rang all too loudly. "Mother of God, don't let me die!"

The starship gave a convulsive shudder and the lights failed completely, plunging the cargo bay into total darkness.

EIGHT

MICHAEL RALSTON OVERCAME his panic almost immediately. He had been in situations like this before, mostly during combat. He remembered the time he had blundered into Westcott's lab, only to find himself tumbling helplessly among the stars because of a bizarre data analysis method the mathematician used.

Ralston's priority lay in finding a bulkhead. Cautiously reaching out to prevent himself from hitting something and beginning an uncontrollable spin, he found the soothing coolness of the composite bulkhead. His groping fingertips lightly brushed along the surface until he came to the ubiquitous elastic cords used for anchoring and propulsion in the zero-gee ship. Ralston tugged and came up against the bulkhead, orienting himself the best he could.

All the while he worked, he heard the pilot cursing volubly.

"I'm anchored. What do I do?" Ralston called out.

"You by the godforsaken control panel?" the pilot demanded.

"Yes, I've got it. What happened?"

"When the alarms went off, I jerked and sent myself off into the hold like some green kid. Dammit!"

"With the ship," said Ralston, trying to keep his anger down. Their lives might be forfeit and all the pilot wanted to do was cover up his embarrassment at drifting in the center of the hold.

The pilot cursed again. Ralston heard a solid *thwack!* that meant the man had finally drifted into a crate. Scratching noises sounded over the still-ringing alarms.

"Talk me in."

"What happened?" Ralston asked again. "You said the redundant systems had gone out. We're not lost between shifts, are we?"

"Got it!" cried the pilot. Ralston felt the pilot pressing close beside him. The man's instinct in the absolute darkness of the hold proved accurate. Ralston heard the pilot working on the panel.

"How serious is it?"

"Serious enough. There." The lights came up slowly. Even so, Ralston squinted and shielded his eyes with a free hand. The pilot continued to work with studied efficiency. The lights returned to their normal level. He finally plucked out the offending block circuit that had burned Ralston's fingers.

"Can you replace it?"

"No problem with that. The problem's in what caused everything to go haywire in the first place." With a casual disregard for the safety of others, the pilot tossed the fused circuit over his shoulder. Ralston watched it tumble away, catching light and reflecting it in rainbows off now-rippled plastic casing. "But we're not."

"Not what?"

"In danger of being lost in mid-shift. We'll exit just fine. I promised we'd come out within ten planetary diameters of Beta 7, and we will. But this . . ." The pilot mumbled again as he worked on the panel. More block circuits followed, to be replaced from a box of spare circuits the pilot pulled from a cache in the wall.

Ralston had begun to relax and watch the man at work when a sizzling sounded. The pilot floated back a meter and stared at his handiwork in disbelief.

"Something's badly wrong with the circuitry. Bet that burned their toast in the galley. Be a while getting this fixed. You want to drift around and watch or do you have something else to be doing?"

Ralston knew when he was being dismissed. He muttered

something and left the cargo hold, taking with him the block circuits from his supervisor to program them. Halfway up the tube he saw Leonore Disa.

"What's wrong, Michael?" she asked. "The lights came back on in parts of the ship. The rest is still dark."

"The pilot's working on it." Ralston didn't try to hide the worry in his voice. "He seems competent enough but the ship acts as if it's on its last legs."

"Nels wasn't able to get any better on such short notice. The pilot came highly recommended, though."

"They're all tinkerers. He'll get the lighting and the rest into shape soon." Ralston had only minimal faith in the pilot's abilities. Over the next week, the lights or the air circulation fans or the heat radiators periodically went out. Only into the third week did the pilot seem to have the problems under control. By the eighth week Ralston had forgotten their early troubles and concentrated on the notes he'd taken during the prior meeting with the Beta 7 native. Once more they would speak with it in an attempt to gain information and to give the warning about the Beta primary going nova.

The senses-ripping transition back into normal space left Michael Ralston stunned for several minutes. Again he experienced the mingling of one sense with another. For a few seconds he thought that he had gone blind, but it proved only a momentary dimming of the ship's lights. The pilot's careful work hadn't been as perfect as he'd bragged. But the lights came back on strongly.

"Everyone in good shape?" called out Nels Bernssen. The blond man drifted to the center of the lounge and slowly rotated, studying those in his expedition. Leonore Disa he knew had come through the shift. The only two requiring assistance were Ralston and Westcott.

The mathematician had struck his head against a wall and damaged the IR sensor. He complained of headaches from this and a ragged flow of information from the ship's computer. Bernssen motioned for one of his technicians to fix the damage.

"Now that we've got our big problem fixed," Bernssen said, looking Ralston over, "how's the minor one? You're pale and your hands are shaking like a bistable vibrator. Want to plug into the automedic and let it check you out?"

"I'm all right," said Ralston, wishing he meant it. "Each transition is a bit harder than the last. I don't believe West-cott's explanation that I'm more susceptible because of the chaos field's residual effects, but what's going on in my head *is* chaotic." Ralston managed a smile that fooled no one.

"The pilot's as good as his word," said Leonore. "He dropped us within ten diameters of Beta 7."

"I wish his repair work was as good as his navigating. The entire ship's going to fall apart at any second," said Ralston.

"I've had some of my people working with him. The pilot wasn't happy about it but we had a long discussion on this point. There were some problems in the control block circuit programming but we've worked through them. The redundant systems are functioning and there's no cause for worry."

Ralston still worried. He'd seen the lights dim at the shift. What else might go wrong?

"I've got the outer moon sighted in, Michael," said Leonore. "We won't be able to land there again, even for a short while, but I'm sending down a dozen automated probes to collect data. Have you looked over their programming?"

"Checked it out a few hours ago. Not what I'd have the probes looking for, but it'll do."

"Any way we can retrieve the probes when they're done? I hate losing this many before we even find the chaos device." Leonore pushed a strand of her lank hair back under a head-band. The concentration on her face made her appear years older. Ralston's mind wandered as he remembered the first expedition he'd commanded. Had he looked this intense? Probably. The responsibility for equipment and personnel— and success—was great. Not having this pressure on his shoulders made the trip more enjoyable for him, but still Ralston envied Leonore.

The head of the expedition chose the study topics. Leonore's interest lay more in calligraphy and visual communication than did his. She had done wonders analyzing the records left by the Alphans, but Ralston thought this missed the true grandeur of that sad, lost race. The telepathic projector was the Alphans' true accomplishment. What factors had gone into the discovery and invention of that process? Although Ralston was no physicist, he needed to know to get a better idea of how the Alphans worked and built and what they expected from their lives.

Of the Betans, they had even sketchier information. A quick landing on the outer moon of Beta 7 had allowed them to use a native-built communication station for a few minutes. The contact had been maddening in its brevity. A xenobiologist would have wanted intimate contact with the Betans; that wasn't possible under ten atmospheres of pressure. A xeno-sociologist needed more data about the beings and their inter-action; Ralston had discovered one self-proclaimed insane individual. None of the other Betans would even speak with them. So much about these people would go unexamined.

The entire Beta system would disappear in the fiery flash from their primary going nova in less than a year.

"I've got everyone hard at work," said Bernssen. "The ship's hull is positively bristling with equipment. Although it would be nice to get much closer to the star, I think we can get good data on the instability and its progress."

"Is the Bernssen Condition fully met yet?" asked Ralston, referring to the theoretical conditions at which the primary would explode. Bernssen had been the first to identify the chaotically induced process in main sequence stars. The pass-ing chaos device had altered the stellar furnace's normal functioning subtly—and enough to cause a nova within a few hundred years.

This star had progressed enough toward destruction that Bernssen estimated only months of life left it as a stable G-class star.

"We're picking up enough instability to set a date," said Bernssen. "Westcott's working on it now."

"Forty-seven standard days, fourteen hours, and a few minutes," came the mathematician's cold answer. "I am unable to determine the time more precisely. The equations diverge more slowly and produce more uncertainty than those for radioactive decay. If you can obtain more precise boundary conditions . . .''

Ralston turned away and left Bernssen and Westcott together. He had little interest in the details. Knowing that this entire solar system would be superheated gas in only forty-seven days depressed him. Not only would countless lives on Beta 7 be lost, but the final refuge of the fleeing Alphans on Beta 5 would also be destroyed. Nothing of the Alphan culture would remain in the universe. An entire world with living, breathing, feeling creatures had been snuffed out. Now the final vestige of that intelligence would disappear completely.

All that was known of the avian Alphans had been collected by his pitiful expeditions.

"There they go," said Leonore. She pointed to a small viewscreen showing a radar return. The tiny blip sank toward the surface of the moon and landed. She turned to the supervisor and began making needless minute adjustments on the controls.

"The programming is fine. Let it work. We can get a readout as the probes spread out to explore," said Ralston. He understood her nervousness. This was the first time she was in command, and she wanted everything to go smoothly.

"Here comes the first signal. I'm putting most of the effort into visual. Those walls with the murals? Remember them? I want closer examination."

Ralston floated away until the lower air pressure in the lounge built a tiny bubble of silence around him. Throughout the large room men and women worked feverishly. Their time here would be limited. The astrophysicists watched the last days of a star before its fiery death. None wanted to miss a single clue to the chaos device's effect on the fusion process.

Westcott correlated data and worked through his intricate equations governing chaos. Ralston felt alone, adrift at the thought. Equations that predicted random behavior. That seemed to be a contradiction, but then he didn't understand the mathematics at all. He'd been told that quantum level effects were statistically predictable, but that wasn't the same thing. Not in his mind, it wasn't.

He rotated to look at the ship's viewscreen. The pilot had shifted the camera to Beta 7 itself. The gas giant showed the typical green, red, and brown bands across its surface. No major cyclonic storms wracked the planet, but Ralston guessed that one or more would become visible if they watched long enough.

"Any contact with their computer yet?" asked Ralston. He hovered close to Leonore's shoulder again. The last time they had been on this moon, Westcott had linked himself directly to an alien machine that allowed the communication and translation with the single being below willing to speak with them.

"Probe 9 looks like it's got contact. Verd, there it is!" Leonore's voice almost cracked with excitement. "We've got a patch through now to the supervisor." She looked over her shoulder at Ralston and said in a low voice, "Do you think Westcott will link up again? It might be our only way of contacting them."

"I'll ask."

Ralston cursed himself for not having thought of this earlier. Westcott had not liked the linkage before and Ralston saw no reason for the man to seek out another bout of brain-searing contact. He should have been cajoling Westcott throughout the trip. There'd been ample time. Ralston sighed and resigned himself to simply not caring for Westcott's company. The computer-brain linkage made the mathematician too strange for Ralston's liking.

"Westcott," he said, hardly wanting to disturb the man now. He had no idea what Nels and the others fed into Westcott's brain for computation. Watery eyes opened and fixed on Ralston.

"I wondered if you would ask."

This startled Ralston. He had thought Westcott lived in his own world, a world distant from reality. That the man understood showed more sensitivity than Ralston had given him credit for.

"I have to. We can get information from the machinery— and we are—but only you can reach the inhabitants again. We need more information. Both Nels and us."

"Bernssen mentioned this. He wants full data on what the Betan called the 'cometary object.' That is how he-she-it saw the chaos field as it passed through the system."

"Then you'll link minds with their computer? I don't know how to thank you."

"I'll find a way," said Westcott in his smug, superior tone. The mathematician kicked free and awkwardly swam to where Leonore worked at the supervisor console. All twelve probes returned a full information stream; she barely kept up with monitoring it.

"He's ready, Leonore," said Ralston.

Her face brightened. "We've used the probe arm to press what we think is the summons button." Huge buttons constituted the major control switches on the alien computer. "If I'm reading our reports correctly, the Betan is trying to respond."

Hesitantly, Leonore moved from the console and allowed Westcott to plug his remote IR sensor into one side. He spent a few minutes adjusting, then said, "I'm ready. Be sure to record everything that is said and done."

"Do you want the automedic standing by?" asked Ralston. He remembered how Westcott had gone into shock on the prior contact.

"Not needed. This time I've built in a filter circuit. I'm not rooting about like some primitive this time. I have the resources of the ship at my command, even if the onboard computer isn't of a significant size."

Westcott touched the toggle switch, hesitated for dramatic effect, then flipped it. Ralston thought the man had accidentally run a killing current through his body. Westcott stiffened and jerked so hard that he began to rotate away. Both Ralston and Leonore grabbed him to maintain the infrared linkage. Westcott's body trembled and his lips moved. No words came out.

"Tell us about it, Westcott. Don't forget that you're safe," said Leonore. "Everything's working out fine." Even as she spoke, she motioned to Bernssen to get the small medical unit. Several of Bernssen's technicians would have to bring it from its storage room since it wasn't mobile in freefall.

"I recognize you," Westcott said in a voice totally unlike his normal tone. "Aberrants! You are the alien aberrants who visited my moon before."

Ralston fought to hold Westcott in position to maintain the infrared link. He hadn't thought it necessary to strap the man down. Leonore lent what help she could but her attention turned more and more to the supervisor controlling the probes exploring the alien base on the moon.

Westcott made choking noises and began frothing at the mouth. Ralston almost reached up to block the beam and cut the mathematician off from this brain-computer-alien linkage, but Westcott batted his hand away. Through lips turned bloody from biting, the man's curt words stopped Ralston. "It's all right. Verd, it's all right. I *need* this creature's information for the equations."

As he spoke, Westcott stiffened even more and alien words spewed from his lips. "The cometary object? Again you ask. I know so little of it. Only a few thousand years ago it came. Or was it a few hundred? It passed by, of that I am certain. Of that and the fact that I am insane. Those I know well. Everyone tells me."

Ralston and Leonore both spoke at the same time. Ralston reluctantly allowed Leonore to ask the questions.

"You have no natural predators?"

"Do we die? Yes, of course. Sometimes a fissioning fails and both parts perish. But only rarely does anyone attempt to fission. Why? Nutrients abound. The air is filled with them."

"Cities?" asked Ralston. "Do you have cities? Buildings to live inside. Machines? What of them?"

"We protect some of our equipment with buildings. But to live? We absorb the air and the food within it. Why hide from it, unless you want to starve to death? Once I tried to kill myself in such a manner. No one cared that I tried, so I gave up on the pursuit. I am quite mad, you realize."

Ralston ran the automedic's probe over Westcott's face and neck, holding it firmly at the base of his skull. The readings on the small auto-doc showed abnormal brainwave activity—nothing Ralston hadn't guessed. How much of this conversation came from the creature on the surface of Beta 7 and how much did Westcott supply? Many concepts had no common ground between things of such diverse bodily forms. Did Westcott interpolate and supply what should be said or what he *thought* should be said?

Only careful analysis afterward would give a clue.

"We need the data on the chaos machine, Michael," came Bernssen's urgent request. "You couldn't maintain contact long before. We dare not miss this chance."

"Westcott," Ralston whispered into the man's ear, "get all the data on the chaos device—the 'cometary object.' All of it! Now!"

Westcott drooled a mixture of blood and saliva down his chin. Ralston wiped it away. When the mathematician attempted to jerk free, both Leonore and Nels held him in place. Ralston regretted this; what torture built in the man's head? Did his body seek to escape while they held him? Was there a brain left after this forced contact?

"They are taking me away. They have decided I am a disruptive influence. Curiosity is aberrant behavior and I am curious. I seek to know everything. The cometary object was only a part of it. I am lost, oh, I am lost to their sanity!"

Westcott sagged.

"Kill the connection," Ralston snapped. Bernssen flicked the toggle while Leonore brought the automedic up to work on Westcott. They guided the unconscious mathematician to a bulkhead and fastened him down. Beside him they attached the auto-doc. Its lights flashed in brilliant, marching sequences as it worked to sedate and cure a condition that might lie beyond its capacity.

"Do you think he was hurt? Permanently, I mean?" asked Leonore. "The last time might have prepared him for this."

"Does he look prepared?" asked Bernssen, his words critical. "He'd better have gotten the data we need. How long before he'll be able to talk?"

Ralston looked at the readouts on the automedic and shook his head. "Can't tell for certain. Nothing here looks familiar. It's working overtime to help him."

"Can we get the information through his IR link?" asked Bernssen.

"Why the rush?" asked Ralston, angry at the physicist for his callousness toward Westcott. Westcott might do little to inspire friendship but what Bernssen proposed might actually damage the man's brain permanently.

"McGhee just finished the first pass on the spectrometer. Your genius made a mistake with his forty-seven days. We might be lucky to have forty-seven hours. If he didn't get the information this time, we might never get it."

Ralston and Leonore exchanged bleak looks. Again the nova would rob them of their find—and again it would destroy an entire planet of intelligent beings.

NINE

"THERE IS LITTLE time left before the sun explodes," said Nels Bernssen. "The changes in the spectrum show it. No doubt," he added, cutting off Ralston's protest.

"What went wrong with Westcott's calculations? We were supposed to have more than a month." Ralston had slipped both arms through elastic bands and looked as if he wore the entire starship as a knapsack. "How could he be so wrong?"

Bernssen shrugged. "You'll have to ask him. My guess is that he didn't use the proper parameters for the boundary conditions. We're dealing with minute quantities, Michael. The slightest change can upset everything."

Ralston remembered Westcott telling of the absurdly delicate balance in nature, how a butterfly's minute wingbeat might produce a severe thunderstorm. The chaos equations allowed for tiny effects to cause immense results.

"How is Westcott?" Ralston asked. Leonore looked worried.

"He's worse than he was before. This time we have the auto-doc handy. I'm not sure what it can really do, though, since the trouble is mental and not physical. The shock of linking brain to brain with the alien has driven him into a coma. The auto-doc keeps his body running but there's no way I can tell when he'll come out."

"We should have brought a medical doctor to handle this. We knew it'd happen."

Even as he complained, Ralston knew this wasn't possible. Every member of this expedition was a specialist, an expert in a narrow field. The automated medical unit was capable of handling almost all accidents and injuries that might occur. The more complex problems might not be handled by a human doctor, either. The human doctor would have been a needless luxury on a flight requiring tight controls on weight and membership.

What Westcott needed more than anything else was a good clinically trained psychologist.

"We're looking at hours, not months," said Bernssen. "I've alerted the pilot to be ready to star out."

"Where?" asked Ralston. "Unless we confirm the data we got before, where do we shift to find the chaos device? Westcott was wrong about the nova's timetable for explosion. He might be wrong about the device's trajectory, too."

"We can't stay here," Bernssen pointed out.

"We might have to. For a while," said the pilot. The man had drifted up and came to a halt in midair without seeming to touch anything. Ralston marveled at his control—and felt his heart almost stop when the pilot's words sank into his churning mind.

"What do you mean we're going to be here for a while?" demanded Ralston. "Didn't you hear Nels? The star's going to blow up at any instant."

"More trouble with the electrical system. We can probably shift with it not working to one hundred percent, but I don't want to try it. This time we might not come out of the shift." The pilot got a pensive look and said, "Wonder what it's like being caught permanently between shifts? Had a math prof in school who tried to figure it out. The math is strange; infinite speed over infinite distance, but the infinities don't match, so that's why we get anywhere. Imagine traveling at infinite speed for infinite time and never going anywhere."

"This is not funny," snapped Leonore. "Are you trying to scare us?"

"Scare you? Why should I? You people seem to do enough scary things to yourselves." He glanced at Westcott, who hung like a bug in a spiderweb. A tiny bead of blood hung at the corner of a bitten lip. Westcott looked more dead than alive.

"If you're not ready to shift away from the Beta system within two days, it might not matter," said Ralston.

"Verd, you told me. The sun's going to go *pop!* at any instant. Puts a bit of pressure on me to fix the old ship, doesn't it?" The man's tone didn't tell of any pressure. If anything, he seemed to be enjoying the prospect of becoming a nova-generated plasma floating outward from this system at sublight speed.

"Talking about it won't get it done," said Leonore. "Do you need help? I'm sure I could find fifteen people in Nels' group to help and two in ours." She exchanged glances with Ralston, who nodded.

"What if I need him?" The pilot pointed at Westcott. The mathematician continued to drool.

"We can use some stimulants to see if this brings him out of shock," suggested Ralston.

"You'd do that just to help? Touching, very touching. You people really are nice, no matter what the other pilots say. Don't bother with him. I'll see what can be done on my own. You just keep peering at the sun and let me know if anything changes."

With that, the pilot drifted off, unconcerned about their fate.

"Why is he like that?" asked Leonore. "He doesn't care if he lives or dies—and he doesn't care if we do, either!"

"Pilots think it's courageous to act like damn fools," said Bernssen. "Never saw one who'd admit to being afraid in any situation. I'm going to send all my technicians to help him. We need this ship in good condition, whether we chase the chaos device or simply go back to Novo Terra." Bernssen licked his lips and ran a quick, nervous hand through a shock of unruly blond hair. Ralston saw that the idea of being trapped in mid-shift didn't appeal to the physicist any more than it did to anyone, except for their pilot.

"Can you plot a trajectory for us, using the data we obtained last time?" asked Ralston. "That way we might be heading in the general direction of the chaos device when we leave this system. We can fine-tune our shift later."

"In spite of Westcott's protests to the contrary, I don't know which way the field traveled. Did it orbit in—for reference let's call it the left—and exit on the right side of the system? Or did it come from the right and go left?''

"I thought he'd established the course from the path of novas it left behind." Ralston uncovered lost civilizations. This type of argument was more alien to him than the cultures he pieced together from physical evidence.

"There's evidence it might have been either. Complete symmetry. Reversal." Bernssen began mumbling. Then, louder, he said, "I talked with Dr. Chen about the survey probes he lost in the Crab Nebula—the 1056 'guest star' he was investigating. The time frame is wrong if the chaos device left this system and then triggered instability in the 1056. It might not be any better if we assume the field passed in the opposite manner."

"You're saying that we don't know whether to go left or right when we leave the Beta system," said Ralston, despair clutching at him. Again, he felt as if he lost everything that he'd worked so long and hard to achieve.

"Westcott might have the information. Or he might not have gained any more than we knew previously. Only he can answer that." Bernssen and Ralston turned to the mathematician. He hung limply in the safety harness, appearing more dead than alive.

"Unless the pilot fixes the ship, we might not be able to go in any direction," said Leonore.

Each floated away in a different direction, cloaked in their own dark thoughts. Fourteen hours later, McGhee gave the warning of intense solar flares. In sixteen, Bernssen warned that they had only minutes before the star exploded. In twenty, the pilot shifted them along the orbit followed by the chaos device, choosing direction at random.

In forty hours, Michael Ralston knew they were in serious trouble.

"Never seen anything like it," the pilot said. The man appeared unruffled by the catastrophe that had stranded them between shifts. "It's almost as if God's hand reached out and squeezed down. The gyroscope just blew itself apart."

The starship's gyroscope provided a vital function in the precision alignment needed for the ship to precisely span light years. The slightest quaver in the ship at the time of starring magnified into huge errors in arrival.

"What happened to it?" asked Ralston. "The 'scope's encased, isn't it?"

"Nothing happened to it, as far as I can see. I've been a pilot for almost eight years and never heard of this happening. The circuitry failed and the gyroscope wobbled. I can't tell you how that's possible. At the speed it rotates, it should have taken a year to slow down enough to wobble like it did." The pilot scratched himself, then smiled. "I guess I'd better get to work figuring out how to fix it. Without a machine shop aboard, I don't see much way. You folks don't happen to have a complete set of machine tools I can use, do you? I didn't think so."

The pilot kicked free and headed down toward the storage area. All Ralston could do was numbly watch him go.

"Happy son of a bitch, isn't he? Does he think God will pluck us out of shift and drop us where we want?" Leonore Disa's bitterness hid her fright.

"He might think that very thing." said Bernssen. "Pilots aren't ordinarily logical, and this one's more gregarious than any of the others I've met."

"Without the 'scope, we might not be able to reenter," said Ralston. "There's no way for the shift engine to perform accurately if we're not lined up right."

"We can get out," said Bernssen. "That's not the problem. Where we end up is. All that talk about varying sizes of infinities is an imprecise way of stating it. Westcott can do better." Ralston, Nels, and Leonore all turned to look at the mathematician. He still hung in his harness, oblivious to the disaster unfolding around him.

"You're saying we can get out, but we won't know where. Is that it?" asked Ralston.

"We might end up a million light years away—or we might drop out of shift in the center of a sun. That's never happened. I doubt we'd do much to the sun. The best that can be said is that we'd never know what happened."

"So we'd be no better off than if we stayed in the Beta system and let the nova take us." Leonore's bitterness carried an even harsher brittle edge now.

"We're still alive," said Bernssen. He made it sound like a curse.

"Can the pilot fix the gyroscope?" asked Ralston.

Bernssen shook his head. "From the sound of it, there's no way of making one precise enough, even if we had the equipment. It takes a carefully programmed lathe just to rough out the body for the spinning mass. Lasers hone it down to within a thousandth of a micron. Even the mass of a partial fingerprint on the surface would throw it out of balance—that's why the disks are sealed in a vacuum a hundred times harder than interstellar space." Bernssen closed his eyes. "A vacuum of less than one atom per hundred cubic centimeters. How do we duplicate that, even if we had the rest of the equipment?"

"The presence of any more atoms would throw off the spinning?" asked Ralston.

"Probably."

"We're dead," Leonore said in a monotone. "We're not going to survive this, are we, Nels?"

"I don't see how," the man answered. He swam to her. They left the lounge. Ralston watched them go, heavy of heart. Their lives should have been ahead.

Anger replaced the self-pity. *His* life still lay ahead! He refused to quietly die. He had been robbed too many times of real fame. The chaos device had taken entire systems in the wink of a nova's eruption. He had lived aboard weightless starships, taking the dozens of foul-tasting drugs that kept the calcium from leaching from his bones, his muscles from atrophying, his vision from fogging, his cells from surrendering to the radiations from the shift engines. He had suffered through all this and for what?

To die without trace between the stars? No!

Ralston knew nothing of the mechanisms involved in running the starship or the physics governing them, but he knew who did. With a deft midair twist, he faced Westcott. The automedic purred quietly as it kept a steady stream of nutrients flowing through the comatose mathematician's body.

Ralston tapped in a new regimen of drugs. Red lights protested this drastic change in therapy. He pushed the override button, then threw two safety toggles and for a final time hit the override. What he did to Westcott he did with full knowledge. Westcott might die from the stimulants surging through his bloodstream, but so what if he did? Would he be any worse off than the others aboard? His death would be a quick, peaceful one.

"To never know," muttered Ralston. Westcott's death might be for the best. He wouldn't spend long weeks anticipating death.

But Michael Ralston could never see Westcott doing such a thing, even if he knew. Westcott was scarcely human. What emotions he still possessed were egocentric. Seldom had Ralston seen a man so totally self-involved and isolated from those around him.

Perhaps that was what made Westcott such a phenomenal theoretician. Ralston didn't care to delve into epistemology.

"Come on, Westcott, snap out of it." Ralston restrained himself from shaking the man or banging his head against the ship's hull. The reward for his control came almost immediately. Westcott's eyelids fluttered and pale, watery eyes struggled to focus.

"They know and they don't care," Westcott said, his voice weak and distant. "They don't care that the primary is going to explode. Danger is an alien concept to them."

"Westcott, we're in trouble. We left the Beta system almost two days ago. Our ship's gyroscopic control is out. We can't accurately shift back."

"Such precision," Westcott went on, as if he hadn't heard. "The creature I spoke with had plotted the chaos field's progression through the system with incredible precision. Such a masterwork. And even he doesn't care that they'll die!"

"The 'scope, Westcott, we've lost our gyroscope."

Westcott's eyes focused and he took in more of the world around him and thought less of what had been burned into his brain by the alien contact.

"The pilot shifted with a bad gyro?" he asked.

"It blew apart after the shift."

"Impossible. It can't happen." Westcott frowned. "Why did we shift? Only I have the precise information needed to find the chaos device."

"The star went nova ahead of schedule. Your calculations

were off.'' Ralston took a savage glee in revealing this to the mathematician. ''We had less than—''

''Uncertainty,'' cried Westcott. ''We returned to the system and introduced a new element of uncertainty by our presence.''

''I know, I know. The butterfly causing the thunderstorm,'' said Ralston.

''It doesn't *cause* anything. It adds a new parameter to the system and creates nonlinear change. The equations change, the result diverges or converges at a new and different rate. I must study this.''

''Go on, since it'll be the last work you ever do.''

''The gyroscope,'' said Westcott, forcing himself back to more practical concerns. ''That fool of a pilot ruined the gyroscope.'' Westcott blinked and fought against the restraining harness. Ralston checked the readout on the auto-doc and decided that Westcott, although still not functioning at optimal, was out of danger and no longer required the chemicals pumping into his body.

As Ralston unhooked the IVs, Westcott said excitedly, ''The residual chaotic effect! It must be that. In rapidly rotating systems the effect might be more pronounced.''

''It didn't affect the other ships in earlier expeditions,'' pointed out Ralston.

''Do you know? Who thought to check? This gyroscope might—never mind all that. Is the gyro completely destroyed?''

Ralston couldn't force the words from his lips. He nodded.

''Leave,'' said Westcott. ''I need to be alone. No, no, you idiot. Don't turn off my IR link with the computer. There's something I can—almost—remember. It must be in the data banks. It must!''

Westcott got the glassy stare when he linked fully with the ship's computer. Ralston wondered at the direct-connect so soon after coming out of shock, but he pushed the thought away. Nothing Westcott could do to himself was worse than what would happen if he didn't come up with something.

Ralston even allowed himself a ray of hope to shine through the bleakness. Westcott was a genius. He might not like the mathematician, but Westcott worked at a level few in the universe did.

"Wait!" called out Westcott. "I have it. Yes, it's there. Obscure, very obscure, but it is so elegant!"

"You can repair the gyroscope?" Ralston hardly believed his ears.

"Repair it? Who wants to? I can design a better one. Why hasn't anyone done this before?"

"So you design a new one," said Ralston, hope fading again. "We don't have the machining tools to manufacture it."

"This requires only simple electronics. Yes, an electronic gyroscope at least a full order of magnitude more accurate. It's possible. It *is* possible!"

"Let me get the pilot. And Nels. And some of his technicians!" Ralston hit a call button and assembled them within a few minutes. The pilot was the last to arrive, indolently floating in, as if this meant little to him.

"What do you need from me?" the pilot asked.

"Your attention. Listen to what Westcott's come up with."

The mathematician hardly noticed the others. He warmed to his topic, thinking aloud. "The Sagnac effect. I knew it but had forgotten. Why remember when the computer stores everything perfectly? The computer has only sketchy information, but we can use its information to build a new gyroscope. And one with true elegance."

"Never heard of this Sagnac effect," said Bernssen. He looked around. Ralston's heart turned to ice when he saw that none of the physicists had heard of it, either. In such an assembly of talent, Ralston thought, at least one should know what Westcott hinted at.

"We need a length of birefringent fiber optic," said Westcott.

"I've got a kilometer or more in the hold," said one scientist. "Want me to get it?"

Westcott motioned him on his way. "And lasers. Several tuned to different frequencies."

"We've got enough tunable continuous wave lasers on-board to open a secondhand store," said Bernssen.

"I use one to heat my meals," said the pilot, still not interested in Westcott. "I don't see what all this is leading to."

"In the birefringent fiber, the light is polarized in different directions and travels at different speeds to produce an interference effect.''

''So?'' asked the pilot. But Ralston noticed that the man's eyes had hardened. Westcott now had undivided attention.

''Change the birefringence and the interference pattern changes,'' said Westcott. ''Make loops of the fiber, send laser beams both clockwise and counterclockwise. Any rotation of the loop will change the relationship between the two beams and . . .''

''And change the interference pattern. So all we do is put an interferometer on the pattern, hook this into the computer, and let it align the ship. No more need of doing it mechanically. We can do it all electronically. I got to say that this is a righteous scheme. I do hope it works.''

''You think it won't?'' asked Ralston.

''I didn't say that. I think it sounds good, but one thing I've learned, nothing ever works quite right.''

''Take a look at the way you've maintained this ship and you can come to that conclusion,'' muttered Bernssen.

''You can walk home,'' the pilot said without animosity. ''I got to do some rigging. You got the fiber optic? Then I want to get to work. I figure it'll take a week or two of programming to get this into the computer.''

''I can do it in only a few hours,'' said Westcott. The sensor atop his skull gleamed a dull silver like a badge of honor.

''I won't argue that. Get to it, Doctor. And the rest of you want to build the new gyro? That looks like it's more in your field than in mine. But I insist on doing the connections for the actual control. This ship is mine.''

Ralston watched the assembled scientists go off in tight knots of two and three to discuss what had to be done. Hollow inside from the strain, Ralston relaxed and floated in mid-room.

Leonore came over to join him. ''Not much we can do, is there?'' she said.

''Makes you feel useless,'' Ralston agreed. ''I don't know anything about optics or Sagnac effects or any of what they're talking over.''

''Nels does. We're lucky to be aboard a research ship

where the people know instrumentation, lasers, optics, all that.''

"Who knows?" said Ralston. "We might get the chance to pay them back using *our* specialty. When we find the chaos device, all their rules are gone. We're used to putting together puzzle pieces in ways no one's ever considered.''

"Do you think we'll get the chance?" asked Leonore.

He took her hand and squeezed. Ralston didn't know the answer to that. The laser-optic gyroscope might work and save them.

Or it might fail and leave them stranded forever.

TEN

"CAN'T WE TEST it first, before trusting it too much?" asked Michael Ralston. "It's risky simply . . . trusting it." He looked at the pile of equipment with growing skepticism. Bernssen had attached an interferometer—this was the only portion of the equipment that Ralston recognized. The rest appeared to be hidden by coils of the fiber optic cable, leads running to the lasers and ship's computer and other devices Ralston couldn't begin to identify.

"How do you propose to test it, Doctor?" Westcott asked acerbically. "It will work. I see nothing wrong with the principle or construction."

"And you were the one who said we'd have almost two months to study Beta 7 and its inhabitants," snapped Ralston.

"I've explained that. Our return to the system changed the boundary conditions. This is different."

Ralston didn't see that, but he kept his peace. Nels Bernssen and the others waited nervously to see if this solid state gyroscope worked. Ralston prayed that it would. For all their sakes.

And for the sake of those who might be touched by the chaos device unless they found and stopped it. Westcott might say it was decaying, falling apart under its own effects, but Ralston had no confidence in the mathematician's predictions now. More variables entered the equations daily, possibly changing the lifetime of the chaos device to centuries or even millennia—or perhaps Westcott had ignored one tiny factor.

When minutiae magnified into star-killing, world-wrecking ability, a small parameter could mean a great deal.

"It's got to work," said Nels. "What choice do we have?" The physicist's arm circled Leonore Disa's waist and drew the small woman close.

Ralston agreed reluctantly. They had no option other than to trust this untried device with their lives. Bernssen had said the shift back into normal space wouldn't be difficult. Where they might end up presented the true problem. And if the gyroscopic alignment system failed in any way, they might be thousands of light years from human-inhabited systems with no way to find their way home.

Ralston screamed as the shift grabbed his senses and shook. Reds burned his tongue and yellows screamed in his ears. Smell turned into a spectrum of color and the tang of ozone from the electrical equipment could be heard ringing throughout the ship.

Tucked into a fetal ball, Ralston rolled over and over in the middle of the chamber. Only when hands reached out and slowed his rotation, did he uncurl to see everything around him appearing normal. His eyes shot toward the viewscreen, but he couldn't tell anything from the star patterns.

"Looks strange," murmured Bernssen. "I don't think this is where we intended to go, but we're not lost. Look," he said to one of his team. "That's a portion of the open star cluster we checked out a year or so back. And over there's Albierio, only slightly distorted. I recognize the gold and blue stars."

"We dropped into real space just fine, ladies and gentleman," came the pilot's cheerful voice over the intercom. "We missed our target but landed at the edge of Nex-controlled space. Blind luck, I call it, but we're less than a week's ordinary travel from Upsilon Hydra 3, or Tosoll as the snakes call it."

Ralston didn't even react when the pilot called the Nex snakes. The relief he felt was too great to take offense at any racial slur. He had been to Tosoll before; he had fought on Tosoll no fewer than three times. Part of the Nex-P'torra settlement had been to allow the Nex full colonization rights to the world. They would be able to find a replacement for their gyroscope and do complete repairs.

"Tosoll's a major base for the Nex," he told Leonore. "Everything's all right now."

Even as he spoke, the pilot increased magnification on the viewscreen and he saw that luck had given them a nearby planet—and luck had also placed them in the center of an invasion fleet.

A P'torra invasion fleet.

"They still haven't detected us," said Ralston. He studied the readouts in the cockpit. It had been many years since he'd worried over such things, but he was the only one aboard the research ship with any military experience. "When they shifted to the Tosoll system, they came out in disarray. Just enough to lose formation. If they keep com silence, we can cruise along with them to Tosoll."

"And then what do we do?" asked the pilot. "By all the saints, I haven't got a clue why you didn't want me contacting the P'torra fleet commander. They're like we are. They'd lend us the equipment we need. I'm sure of it."

Ralston didn't want to start the old argument anew. He had convinced Bernssen that an invasion fleet would destroy without question anyone appearing in the center of their battle cluster. But the pilot had a good point. Should they try to warn the Nex on Tosoll and risk immediate destruction by the warships surrounding them, or should they continue as they were?

When the fleet reached Tosoll, they'd assume preplanned positions and it would become obvious that an extraneous ship toured in the middle where it didn't belong. Any unknown ship had to be the enemy. Ralston could see the P'torra opening fire instantly. Yet trying to hold back while they were still some distance from Tosoll presented problems of its own. What if a P'torra ship pulled alongside to see if they could lend aid to another they thought to be one of their own?

"We're living on borrowed time," said the pilot. "This bollixed together gyro is still working, but we can't hope to go tearing off without replacing it. The St. Dismas-damned thing has to be replaced. I *will* see it replaced, too, or I don't pilot another centimeter after this space gadget of yours.''

"We could send a message rocket down to Tosoll," suggested Leonore. "If the Nex knew the danger coming in on them, the P'torra might break off and leave."

"How likely does that sound?" asked Ralston. "The P'torra have assembled a war fleet. They'd simply accelerate their attack. As it stands, they're spiraling down slowly. We're on the opposite side of the sun from Tosoll right now and the Nex aren't likely to see us until it's too late. Even with a continuous-drive rocket we're not going to get it to Tosoll in time for any meaningful response."

"Do you suppose they're at war again? The Nex and the P'torra?" asked Bernssen.

"It looks that way. Or perhaps the P'torra decided on a sneak attack. A quick thrust, take Tosoll, then consolidate before word can get out. They might be able to take several Nex planets that way before anyone realizes the war has heated up again."

"Michael, you make it sound as if the P'torra are evil." Leonore stared at him. He had to keep reminding himself that the others didn't necessarily share his pro-Nex views. As he'd learned on campus, most of the students and faculty openly opposed him on this issue. Leonore had believed him when he said he killed the P'torra student in self-defense. That didn't mean she accepted his views about them generally with an open mind.

"Those are old questions I've answered for myself. You'll have to do it for yourself." Ralston gestured, taking in all the space around their ship with the arm motion.

"What *are* they doing here?" asked Bernssen. "I can't come up with any answer other than the one Michael's proposed. It looks as if the P'torra are attacking."

"Unprovoked?" asked the pilot. "None of us can say. How do we know that the slimy Nex didn't do something to bring all this down on their pointy heads? By all the saints and Mother Mary, *they're* the ones we can't trust."

"Whoever started it—or will start the war again—we're agreed that alerting the P'torra ships englobing us is suicidal," said Ralston. He watched the pilot's reaction. The pilot had resigned himself to obeying the orders given by Bernssen. And Nels had made it clear to the pilot that they were not to communicate with anyone until he decided.

Ralston motioned for Bernssen and Leonore to talk privately. The three hung in the center of the lounge, isolated from the others.

"Any bright ideas?" asked Bernssen. "I'm tapped out. There doesn't seem any good way for us to declare ourselves neutral."

"We might not be able to, even if we wanted," said Ralston. Seeing the others' expression, he said grimly, "The P'torra threatened me about revealing all I'd discovered about the chaos device. And Slenth offered to finance an expedition. The Nex want control of it."

"It is an interesting—" began Leonore. She covered her mouth with a hand and gasped when the real reason came to her. "They want it as a weapon. They want to turn each other's sun into a nova."

"The Nex would be happy with that," agreed Ralston. "The P'torra might find the notion of giving everyone on a Nex-held planet incurable epilepsy interesting scientifically. Or mutations in the germ plasma. They'd enjoy watching a Nex-inhabited world destroyed by genetic mutation over a hundred years. The P'torra time sense is considerably different from ours. A century of planning to them is about the same as a month is to us."

"I feel I'm hearing only one side of a propaganda broadcast," said Bernssen. "No disrespect meant, Michael, but we know you're prejudiced in this. The P'torra might not be the vile backstabbing bastards you make them out to be."

"We don't have to worry about Michael," spoke up Leonore. "He's here, with us, in an expedition where he's not primary investigator. Doesn't that tell you something, Nels?"

"What?" The blond man frowned, not seeing what Leonore was getting at.

"Michael turned down the Nex offer to finance his own expedition. He doesn't want them to have the secrets locked in the chaos device, either."

Ralston had seldom felt more desolate and lost. "Leonore's

right. Whatever happens, we can't afford to let either side
have the information we gather.''

"Keeping it from them is going to be hard, especially
when my people start publishing papers on the field. Westcott's got a start on solving the equations. When the theoretical work is done—and put with the direct observation of the
device—we might be able to build one ourselves. And anyone
reading our papers can duplicate our work.''

"You're not asking us not to publish, are you, Michael?''
Leonore's eyes blazed in anger at this notion.

"We've got some responsibility, not only to science but to
civilization.''

"Keeping this knowledge to ourselves won't serve any
purpose," said Bernssen. "It will come out. A hint here, a
solid clue there. Both the Nex and the P'torra are highly
advanced. There's no real difference in the level of their
science and ours. We can't be responsible for how they'd
use—or misuse—what we find.''

"We're going back a couple centuries with these arguments, Nels," said Ralston. "Rather than talk them to death
again, let's agree on what we can do. Foremost is to stay
alive. Agreed on that point?''

"You make it sound difficult, Michael," said Leonore.
"I'm not convinced that we can't simply contact the P'torra
commander and declare ourselves neutral and in trouble. Put
out a distress signal and then talk.''

Ralston wanted to scream in frustration. All around them
rocketed warships armed with interceptor missiles capable of
laying waste to a planetary area equal to half the island on
which the University of Ilium stood. Call it fifty thousand
hectares. Call it a million. To Ralston it didn't matter; one of
those missiles could destroy their ship as surely as the nova
that had taken both the Alpha and Beta systems.

Getting Leonore to understand this wouldn't be easy.

"Let's approach this question in a different way," Ralston
said. "Imagine yourself the commander of a P'torra warship.
Like the ones all around. You're keyed up, aren't you? No
matter what's gone on—either the Nex started this or they
didn't—you know that the Nex will destroy you if they get
the chance. Verd?''

"Verd," agreed Leonore.

"You're approaching an enemy-held planet and a strange signal blasts across your com unit. Enemy? It might be since you're under com silence. Or is it a neutral ship? Does it matter? It's endangering your approach and might alert the Nex. Solution: destroy the problem."

"All right, all right, I see the problem. With reservation, I'll go along with doing nothing to contact the P'torra. Where does that leave us?"

"We're scientists. We're used to finding solutions to knotty problems. What are our resources? What can we do in the time we have?" Ralston had answers of his own dealing with contacting the Nex, but the others wouldn't accept them.

"Our equipment," said Bernssen. "We've got a large amount of equipment for studying solar activity."

"Putting together the fiber optic-laser gyroscope shows we can put it together in different ways," said Leonore. "A weapon?"

"No weapons," said Ralston. Both stared at him.

"Why not? I'd have thought you would be the first to advocate firing on the P'torra," said Bernssen.

"No suicide, remember. We're noncombatants and I want to keep it that way, if possible. They outnumber us fifty to one. It's going to be hard enough not being in the middle when the battle starts."

"The point is well taken about them outnumbering us. They're experienced, too, unless I miss a guess," said Nels. "So, no weapons. Studying them isn't going to help us."

"We have something else," said Ralston, not knowing where he went with the idea. "We have knowledge. Both the P'torra and the Nex want what we've found out about the chaos device. How can we use that data to our benefit?"

"As trade?" suggested Leonore. "No, we're agreed that neither side should have that information." The woman's statement surprised Ralston. They hadn't decided that. When Nels tacitly went along, Ralston mentally scored a major victory for himself. "How can we use the knowledge of the chaos device to extricate ourselves?"

"That's a question we should pose to Westcott," Ralston

said. "He's the one with the most intimate knowledge of the chaos equations and potential solutions."

"We can't expect to put together a super-drive and simply leave," said Bernssen. "Likewise, we can't expect some miracle weapon or gadget that'll solve everything for us."

"Why not? Westcott's been working overtime to redeem himself for the mistake in his calculations back in the Beta system."

"That wasn't his fault," said Leonore.

Ralston knew this was true, but an entire planet filled with intelligent beings had perished. Nothing Westcott could have done would have prevented their destruction, but of all those in the expedition, Westcott felt the closest to the inhabitants of Beta 7. Only he had communicated directly with them. He had to feel the loss of untold millions of thinking, if alien, creatures. And he had miscalculated. Although it wasn't logical, Ralston believed that Westcott felt responsible for the Betans' earlier than expected deaths. Just the way the mathematician drove himself hinted at that guilt. Ralston found himself smiling. Westcott might retain more humanity than he had given the man credit for.

"I'll go see what he has to say," offered Ralston. "Why don't you two start asking the others if they have any ideas? It'll be helpful to know where we stand with them."

Nels and Leonore silently left. Ralston heaved a deep sigh. He found himself hoping again, pinning all his faith on Westcott. Saving the expedition might be more than even his genius could deliver.

He found Westcott curled up near the sensor unit mounted on the computer. The slack expression on Westcott's face told Ralston that the mathematician worked constantly with the computer. For a fleeting instant Ralston wondered what it would be like to have instant access to all that information, to be able to retrieve any detail, no matter how obscure and have it a part of you, to calculate faster than any other human, to become more machine than man.

Revulsion replaced curiosity.

"Westcott," Ralston said, shaking the man gently. In freefall this didn't work too well. Ralston planted his feet under conveniently placed braces on the bulkhead and tried again. This time he aroused Westcott from his meditations.

"What?" Westcott's irritability indicated that Ralston might have caused a headache by precipitously breaking the brain-computer infrared link.

"We need you," Ralston said simply.

Westcott blinked. His shaved head reflected light from a nearby lamp. His eyes narrowed, as if expecting this to be a trick. "What do you mean, 'you need me'?"

"Just that." Ralston quickly explained their dilemma. "We need the facilities on Tosoll. If the P'torra fleet continues on course, those facilities might be destroyed or captured. But we can't fight their entire force, nor can we warn the Nex. Doing so would mean sure destruction for us."

"Mathematics does not lend itself to matters of war," said Westcott. "I fail to see how I can aid you."

"The chaos equations," said Ralston, inspiration flowing. "You mentioned once that the equations might describe how wars occur. The dynamics of randomness sets off fights."

"It's possible to develop such a system of equations, but it'd take years to find the proper parameters. What matters? What doesn't? It'd be easier to figure out how the chaos device worked, using the same nonlinear equations."

"It would?" Ralston brightened. "How long would that take?" He had visions of a chaos ray totally destroying the P'torra fleet.

"Couldn't take longer than, say, two years of dedicated work. I would have to be alone, though. No more interruptions."

"Two years!" Ralston exploded. "We need answers *now*."

Westcott only shrugged.

Ralston's mind raced. He refused to let loose of the idea that within this science ship's hull someone had the solution to their survival. Over and over, the thread of his tangled thoughts returned to Westcott.

"You have the system defined for radioactive decay, don't you?" asked Ralston. Westcott nodded. "What happens if you consider the ships around us as atoms, their missiles as, say, alpha particles? Could you decide which was most likely to shoot at us?"

"The answer to that doesn't require complex matrices,"

said Westcott. "The nearest one would fire and destroy us."
Westcott's eyes glazed as he drifted off on a mental tangent. Ralston almost shook the man again but for some reason he couldn't understand allowed the mathematician to continue his thought.

It proved worthwhile.

"There is something, though," said Westcott. "Intriguing idea. Of course the chaos equations describe conditions leading to war. Radioactive decay is another random event. What if I analyzed the trajectory away from the fleet that afforded us the maximum chance for escape and also resulted in maximum confusion among the P'torra? Is there an optimal course that will ram one of their ships into another—several into each other—and let us reach Tosoll before them?"

"Is there?" asked Ralston.

The computer began working hard as Westcott turned to it, his IR sensor linking again with the larger machine. For long minutes, Westcott hung immobile and then turned, a faint smile on his lips.

"There is such a course. We must be able to make corrections constantly, according to the shifting patterns of the P'torra vessels and the probability of destruction from each. However, we must embark soon. And I would need to connect directly with the ship's controls to control the dodging we will undoubtedly need to do."

Ralston slammed his hand against the intercom call button. Reluctance etched in every line of his body, the pilot came from the cockpit to listen to Westcott's scheme.

"By Mother Mary, no!" he roared. "I won't turn over my ship to anyone."

"Even if it means we'll all be killed—and your ship blown out of space." With the last statement Ralston knew he'd caught the pilot's full attention.

"You'll guarantee us getting through?" the pilot asked. "With no damage to the ship?"

"Does it matter what Ralston agreed to?" asked Westcott. "If we are destroyed, it will be after considerable effort. As it stands, we have no hope."

"Do it," said the pilot. "But I'll be at the controls. The first time it looks as if you're chinging it up, I take control and we blast hard for Tosoll."

"Agreed," said Westcott. The pilot left, muttering to himself.

"You'll keep total control, through the computer?" asked Ralston.

"Of course," Westcott said smugly. "Our course will be illogical, contrary to everything he has learned about piloting. We will have to be chaotic in our effort."

Westcott turned and anchored himself firmly, head and IR sensor just centimeters from the receptor unit on the computer. The ship jumped almost instantly. Ralston heard the pilot over the intercom ordering all hands to secure for rapid maneuvering.

Ralston slammed hard into the bulkhead as Westcott turned the ship on its axis, then accelerated all out.

And this was only the beginning of their race.

"Missiles launched," came the pilot's anxious voice. "Mother Mary, here they come. Four of the chinging whoresons!"

Ralston braced for the impact. P'torra missiles never missed their targets. Never.

ELEVEN

WITH EVERY SHARP movement of the ship, Michael Ralston thought they'd been hit by the P'torra missiles. But as far as he could tell, they escaped unscathed. Westcott's precipitous turnings and dodgings produced all the motion within.

"Inertial system," muttered Westcott, hunched close to the IR sensor and the computer. "We can turn quickly enough."

Even as he spoke, Ralston felt as if he'd spun about wildly. The ship lurched under him and slammed him hard into a bulkhead. He struggled to put on a harness and get into the nearest acceleration couch. Even this didn't keep him from bruising shoulders and waist. The couch had been designed for acceleration in one direction. Westcott had the ship dancing and sidestepping to a chaotic tune.

"Pilot's trying to regain control. Won't let him. Won't!" Westcott cackled. Ralston closed his eyes and found this worse than staring at the viewscreen.

A field of stars dotted the screen. None of them appeared to be moving, but Ralston knew this was deceptive. He blinked when two tiny dots moved slowly from left to right across the screen. As suddenly as they appeared, the star field abruptly changed and the dots disappeared. Westcott had accelerated along a new vector to leave behind the deadly missiles.

"We can't outrun their weapons," called Ralston. "Maybe we should surrender."

"No!" bellowed Westcott. Ralston had no idea if the

mathematician was denying the suggestion or responding to some condition picked up by the ship's radar.

From over the intercom came the pilot's frenzied voice. "You've blown out two rockets. We can't make it on the three remaining. Give it up, by all the saints, give it up!"

Westcott had become a part of the ship and its computer. Ralston studied the man and saw no vestige of humanity remaining. Westcott might have been a component plugged into the circuit.

The component performed flawlessly. In the viewscreen came a tiny dot that grew larger with breathtaking rapidity: Tosoll.

"The planet. There's Tosoll! We've gotten through to the planet!" cried Ralston. Even as he recognized the outlines of the continents through the gauzy white cotton of clouds, he knew they'd only succeeded halfway. By now the Nex battle command had been alerted and waited for the invasion fleet.

What ship came blasting down first? The one that had escaped the P'torra fleet. Them.

"Westcott, listen," Ralston cried out. "The Nex will try to blow us apart, too. Evade. Evade anything coming up from the planet!"

"Surveillance units," muttered Westcott. "New variables. New matrix required. Need time. Need time to compute."

Ralston jerked free of the straps which had held him together during the maneuvering. He kicked out and fell heavily. Westcott maintained a steady acceleration now, giving them almost the full Novo Terra gravity. Legs unused to such strain, Ralston fought toward the cockpit. The pilot seemed unaffected by the acceleration—Ralston guessed he was more consistent in taking the medication designed to prevent muscle atrophy caused by prolonged weightlessness.

"I need the com unit. I've got to get in touch with them before they blast us out of space."

"The P'torra or the Nex?" asked the pilot. His eyes had gone as round and glazed as saucers. "Both are turning everything they can on us."

Ralston doubted that. A full planetary defense system would ignore a single ship and let only a few units cope with it. And the P'torra wouldn't have more than one or two ships dispatched to eliminate them. Their primary targets lay below on Tosoll's surface.

"Static, can you get rid of the static?" Ralston demanded of the pilot.

The man shook his head. "I've never seen such intense jamming. Both sides are preventing us from talking."

Ralston understood all too well. The P'torra thought they were a Nex reconnaissance ship. To prevent them from reporting back on fleet strength required sophisticated jamming of all the communication channels. The Nex also tried to prevent them from communicating, because they thought this might be a P'torra advance scout determined to trigger defenses and pinpoint strengths and weaknesses.

"Can we get a lasercom unit working?" Ralston asked.

"There are a dozen still mounted on the hull," said the pilot. "They belong to your team—or to Dr. Bernssen's."

Ralston remembered that Bernssen and the others had monitored the Beta primary across a full electromagnetic spectrum. He left the pilot vainly trying to regain control of his ship. Staggering, Ralston made his way below and found Leonore Disa and Nels Bernssen.

"Nels, I need to use a lasercom. You have one mounted outside that'll go in the right frequency?"

"To contact the Nex?"

"Both sides are jamming the usual channels. We're going to have to punch through the static and find one of their commercial stations and try to overload its pickup with our signal. Both sides will blow us into dust if I don't."

"Don't know how much good this will do, but give it a try." Bernssen painfully worked his way across the cargo hold to where instruments had been shock-mounted on the bulkhead. Only this had saved them from being smashed during Westcott's violent course changes.

Bernssen sighed as he saw the minor damage done. "Have to recalibrate all this. No good for scientific work, but it should give you what you need."

Ralston saw an immediate problem. "How do I hold it on target, should I get lucky enough to find one?"

"Controls are there, but they're for fine-tuning. No gross

movements are allowed. No need when we sight in, it's usually on a star.''

Ralston struggled with the equipment, swinging the lasercom beam back and forth desperately seeking a carrier signal. He found one but the abrupt turnings of the ship prevented him from locking on.

"Want me to see if Westcott can slow down the dodging?" asked Leonore.

"No!" Ralston had some idea of the armament turned against them. To stay on any single vector now without chaotically determined variation meant instant death. "I'll try to do better."

Sweat blinded Ralston as he worked on the lasercom unit. Finally, he found a carrier signal—or it found him.

He didn't care which it was. Ralston began pulsing the laser in the code he had learned while with the Nex. In the intervening years, he was sure they'd changed the code, but Ralston hoped that someone recognized it and would be curious enough to cease firing long enough to establish hard communication.

"Lost it. Damnation!"

The ship rolled, then went into a wild spin that threw Ralston hard into the bulkhead, stunning him. It took long minutes for him to realize that he was still alive and that the most violent of the maneuvers had passed. Ralston picked himself up and wiped away the bloody smear from his forehead where he'd connected with the edge of a crate.

"Nels, Leonore?" he called out. They had been thrown together behind another crate. They lay together, still groggy. He checked to be sure that they hadn't sustained serious injuries, then turned back to the lasercom.

The rapid fluctuations on the power meter indicated complex signals coming along the beam—signals Ralston had no hope of translating without the needed codes.

He slammed his hand against the intercom call button and shouted to the pilot, "Anything on the regular com channels?"

"Orders for a parking orbit," the pilot responded. "Should we trust those snakes?"

"Westcott!" called Ralston, ignoring the pilot. "Follow the Nex instructions. Do you understand?"

"Safety behind their orbiting fortress, yes, yes," said West-cott, his voice distant and strained.

Ralston didn't know what the mathematician muttered about, but he knew any relief from the dangerous maneuvering could only benefit them. Ralston fought his way up the central passageway, being driven to his knees once when Westcott accelerated abruptly. Fighting the black tide of rising uncon-sciousness, Ralston made his way back into the lounge area where Westcott had established his computer link.

A few others had come into the lounge to watch. All had wisely strapped themselves down in acceleration couches.

"What's happening?" he demanded.

"Nex orders to go to a base. A satellite fortress, from the description." Westcott's face had turned gaunt and haggard. No color remained and the man's clothing hung wetly on his skinny frame. His eyes peered at Ralston, with recognition and infinite tiredness. "I didn't think I could do it. But I did!"

"You got us through in one piece," agreed Ralston.

"No, no, not that. The piloting was secondary. The com-putation, man, the computation! The chaos equation matrix had to be solved several times a minute. At one point, I had to solve it every fifteen seconds. So complex. The computing power." Westcott closed his eyes and put his hands on his shaved skull, as if trying to hold in his brains. He stroked the IR sensor as if it were a loved one.

"You did it," repeated Ralston, not understanding but still approving.

"I treated the P'torra ships as if they were atoms trying to decay. I considered this ship as a particle traveling through the lattice structure and sought a path for us that caused maximum interaction." Westcott chuckled. "Four P'torra ships rammed into one another."

"And one shot the other out of the sky," chimed in the pilot. "I saw it on the screen. By the saints, we may not have been armed, but we eliminated a full ten percent of their fleet."

"How badly damaged are we?" asked Ralston.

"The rockets are shot. Try to fire them again and we all go up, *poof!* But the damnedest thing's happened. That Sagnac gyroscope gadget you people put together is still working. Working better than it has any right to. The saints smiled on us this time." The pilot glanced over at the viewscreen. "They smiled then and must be laughing now. We got *them* to deal with. Imagine a snake ordering me to spin the ship so they can come aboard in comfort. Imagine them ordering me to do anything!"

The viewscreen showed small tugs fastening probes to the ship's hull. Ralston knew that the Nex would monitor the internal workings of the ship and be warned if they tried to escape.

"Let their representatives in," ordered Ralston. "I'll talk to them."

"Not unless you can hiss," said the pilot. "Those scale-faces don't speak our language."

Ralston again marveled at the lack of knowledge and the extent of prejudice against the Nex. He waited for the pilot to say something about the Nex looking like expensive luggage, but the comment never came. The man sank down into a silent sulk when the Nex commander and two assistants came through to the lounge.

The scientists noted the heavy energy weapons the Nex carried.

Before any of them could create a problem, Ralston went forward, arms extended and palms upward in the traditional Nex greeting.

"You are to know well of us?" asked their leader. He had thrown back the fragile-appearing hood of his spacesuit. Unlike Slenth, this Nex was gray-scaled. Ralston knew that some status was attached to scale coloration, but he had never determined exactly what it was.

"I wish you long life and victory over your enemies, may they fall from space!"

"Sentiments of goodwill ring nice," said the Nex. "Humans?" The reptile glanced around, but his hard black eyes never strayed far from Ralston.

"We come only in peace. We inadvertently shifted into the middle of the P'torra invasion fleet. We are no allies of the P'torra. We're damaged and need your assistance."

"You are neither of the Nex," snapped the commander.

"I fought with Commander Slenth," said Ralston. "Before that, I fought three campaigns on the surface below. I was there when Tosoll returned to Nex control."

The commander dropped to all fours and scurried around, tasting the air with his long, forked tongue. He rose in front of Ralston, that leathery black tongue whipping about. Ralston didn't stir. He held out his hand again, palm up. The Nex lightly sampled.

"There has talk of you before this."

"I'm Michael Ralston. I've resigned my commission in the Nex Planetary Defense Force and am now a professor at the University of Ilium on Novo Terra. The others are also researchers. We're neutral, not involved in any new dispute with the P'torra."

The Nex whipped about and hissed loudly. Ralston tried to follow the orders flung at the reptile's subordinate but failed. The words came too rapidly and in a dialect with which he wasn't familiar.

"Peaceful mission of seeking?" asked the Nex commander.

"We had our shift alignment gyroscope go out. We tried to replace it and we ended up here by accident. We had no idea that the P'torra were attacking Nex outposts."

"P'torra attack constantly. Vigilance needs always watching for those fish."

"We have no desire to take sides. We wish to remain neutral," said Ralston.

"You, neutral? When is this?"

Ralston struggled with what the Nex meant. "Ever since the war officially ended, I have been neutral in such matters. Politics has lost its appeal."

"You meet Slenth only time short while ago," accused the commander.

"I hadn't seen him in over five years."

"Come with me." When Nels and Leonore started to follow, the commander snapped, "This one only. You stay and be neutral. No danger will harm you."

At the airlock Ralston said, "I'll get my suit on."

"No need. We move through quick-tube."

Ralston uneasily trailed behind the reptile. He noted that the commander had fastened his spacesuit hood against emergencies. The Nex quick-tube connectors between ships were notoriously leaky, but Ralston saw he had little choice. The Nex treated them all as prisoners of war rather than neutral civilians. He couldn't blame them, yet it frustrated him mightily.

The tube creaked and groaned as it flexed to make up the small differences in rotation between the research ship and the small scout docked and orbiting around. Ralston admired the Nex piloting ability, but if they hadn't ordered the ship spun for artificial gravity, there'd have been no need for such fancy work. That was the Nex way. Ralston had never fully understood their desire to do things the hard way when simpler ones were just as good. In a sense, this had been their major obstacle in the war against the P'torra. The Nex chose methods of attack that were needlessly complicated and often did not succeed fully.

In the scout ship, Ralston found an acceleration pad against the rear bulkhead. He fixed himself to it without being told. The Nex drove like wild men. In a combat situation such as this, their maneuvering would be even more spectacular.

Ralston wasn't disappointed. The rapid dodging that took them to the surface of the armored moon left bruises on Ralston's arms, legs, and body where the broad web straps stretched taut.

On shaky legs, Ralston went through the airlock once more. The difference in gravity was all that kept him from falling on his face. This moon's pull amounted to less than ten percent of Novo Terra's. He held himself as erect as possible. To show weakness meant a major breach of etiquette and made it more difficult to successfully present his case of neutrality.

"There," said the commander. "Sit."

Ralston gratefully sank into a cushioned chair that had never been built for the human frame. The sides came in too severely and squeezed at Ralston's hips. His shoulders and upper body found no support, but the way the chair stretched back almost parallel to the floor gave him the chance to lounge enough to rest.

Another gray-scaled Nex entered. Ralston did not stand. He had been offered the chair and, as a guest, he had the right to remain in it. The Nex came over without introduction.

Ralston held out his palm and endured the light, damp flicks of tongue against his flesh.

"Slenth is told me of you." The Nex shook his head slightly, then said, "Slenth *has* told me of you."

"You know Commander Slenth?" asked Ralston.

"His mission to your planet world is of vital importance. You are Ralston doctor." The way the reptile said it left no doubt that they had identified him. Ralston wondered if Slenth had marked him in some fashion. The Nex tongues were incredibly sensitive organs. In spite of scrubbing for space, heavy disinfectants, and almost two months since he'd seen Slenth, some trace of Slenth must remain on his skin.

"I know nothing of his mission. I am neutral now. The P'torra fleet was—"

"This has been explained," said the Nex. "Coincidence occurs. We are glad you arrived."

"The battle," said Ralston. "How is it going? The P'torra seemed to have launched a sneak attack."

"We prepare for any treachery. Your cleverness destroyed five of their vessels. You must tell us of your evasion plan. It will serve us well."

"Luck," insisted Ralston. "Only luck. We are severely damaged and our course proved too erratic for the P'torra to track accurately. Our maneuvering rockets are burned out and we need a new gyroscope before we can continue."

"Continue to what location?" The Nex hunkered down, tiny hands fluttering in front of him like captive birds. Ralston knew this indicated strict attention. The Nex missed nothing in what Ralston said. The archaeologist had to admit that he'd never met a Nex with such a good command of the human language, either.

"We're following a . . . cometary object that passed through a system we've noted as Beta. Most of the expedition staff are astrophysicists interested in examining it."

"What of you? An archaeologist of such fame would not share the physicists' goals. Slenth tells of a discovery of important meaning that you seek."

Excitement caused the Nex to revert to, for him, more natural speech patterns.

"In the Beta system we found ruins that gave some indication about the trajectory of the cometary object. Further, we contacted intelligent beings who lived on a gas giant who had directly observed the object. For this research, I and a former student of mine are required.''

"Slenth hints at greatness in your work. No details have come to such distant outposts, but this maybe might give Nex superior edge over the P'torra?''

"Knowledge is its own reward. We are scientists. We don't look for weapons of war.''

"But this maybe can be changed for this?'' the Nex pressed.

"How knowledge is used is beyond my realm. I am interested only in the civilization that constructed the object we follow.''

"What share might we obtain of your knowledge—in exchange for rocket repair and new gyroscope?''

Ralston had no immediate answer for this. He couldn't promise to reveal to the Nex any information obtained from the chaos device. But they were obviously in the middle of a war situation; the Nex might refuse to give them the equipment or even imprison them until the P'torra had broken off their attack.

Ralston didn't like the idea of being in a Nex jail for years.

"You put me in a bad position,'' Ralston said. "I don't believe I know your name or title.''

"Excuse such bad manners on this one's part. I am Chosinth, Regent of Tosoll.''

"Chosinth, it is my honor. Your fame precedes you.'' Ralston tried to hide his fear. Chosinth had a reputation for viciousness when it came to dealing with the P'torra that even exceeded that of the rest of his cold-blooded race. Ralston had never seen a Nex offer the slightest mercy to a captive P'torra. Chosinth had built a reputation on being even more ruthless.

"I have killed many P'torra, and I will kill many more.'' The Nex ruler of Tosoll opened his mouth and revealed the sharp teeth within in a mocking smile. "With your aid, I will kill many more.''

"How does the battle go?'' Ralston had been straining to hear the defensive arms responding to any attack. No sound of them had come while he'd been with Chosinth.

"They arrived in great disarray. Although we had not expected them, we rallied quickly to defense. Your appearance in their fleet aided us greatly and hindered them. The warning we thank you for. It saved many Nex lives."

"Is this not payment enough for the repairs we need?"

Chosinth hissed in approval. "Your displayed courage in barter confirms Slenth's opinion of you. He spoke well of your battle courage. Your current bravery reflects well on him and you."

"Many lives were saved," Ralston mused. "No one can place a value on a life. A gyroscope? A rocket tube? Who can say?"

"Such might be available, now that the P'torra have run like cravens once again."

"But you want more."

"The chaos weapon you seek. We want it. It will save many, many Nex lives." Chosinth rocked slowly on his powerful hind legs. Ralston read determination in every line of the Nex's body.

"For the reasons I gave Slenth, I can't turn over such data to you."

"I know nothing of what you said to Slenth."

"We will publish scientific papers on our discoveries."

"All can read these. Even the P'torra. We need this weapon before they have it."

"It's impossible for you to send along an observer," Ralston said. "Human feelings against the Nex run high. Even the pilot would refuse to continue in such a case."

"It would place immense burden on the observer, also," said Chosinth. "Your return to Tosoll is impossible to force. You do not command this expedition." The way Chosinth inflected the words told Ralston that the Nex knew just about everything about the organization of the expedition. "Would it be wrong to see before the publication any of your research papers? It is my belief that such practice is not of unusual nature."

"You want a prepublication look at my results?"

"All results. This is price of gyroscope and rockets."

"I could promise and then ignore it later. Or there might

never be a publication. Nothing might work out for the expedition.''

Chosinth again smiled. ''Another human might lie. You have true honor. Your word is sufficient.''

''I can't promise for Bernssen and the others.''

''Ask of them. We will trust in your honor. If you vouch for them, we will trust in theirs, too.''

Ralston worried over the dilemma. They might not find anything of value when they got to the chaos device—they might never even find it. On the other hand, if they unlocked the deadly secrets of chaos it held, giving these to the Nex might be the start of a new and infinitely more deadly war with the P'torra.

He didn't know what to say because Chosinth had him estimated well. Once he gave his word, he wouldn't go back on it. Salazar and the others at the University had stripped him of almost everything he'd spent a lifetime working for. No tenure, no position, cut off from deserved publications. All he had left was his honor.

Damn Chosinth! Damn them all!

TWELVE

"THEY LIED," EXCLAIMED the pilot. "By all the saints, those slimy snakes lied!"

He crossed himself as an explosion caused the ship to shudder. The pilot turned back to the control panel and punched in viewscreen coordinates that showed part of the P'torra battle fleet coming around the bright crescent of Tosoll.

"The Nex said they'd driven off the P'torra. They didn't say they'd stopped the attacks." Even as Michael Ralston watched, trails of two P'torra missiles appeared on the screen. Nex interceptors destroyed both in silent fury.

"The P'torra are dropping most of the missiles in from a dozen A.U.s," said the pilot. "Then there are the ones in orbit around Tosoll. They seem to bombard the surface as much as they bombard us. Really turning the surface to hash." The man's voice carried distaste at the destruction done by the marauding P'torra.

The research ship still clung to the Nex moon base, more dismantled than put together. The pilot agonized over every bolt removed, every piece of delicately calibrated equipment replaced, every slither and hiss made by the efficient Nex workers.

"You don't think they enjoy having the P'torra bomb their planet, do you? If they could, they'd get rid of them in an instant." Ralston fell silent at his own words. The reptiles would destroy the P'torra home world completely, given the chance—given the deadly power of the star-altering chaos weapon. And how could Ralston deny their cause? The P'torra laid waste to hundreds of thousands of hectares on Tosoll's surface. Of the fifty ships in the P'torra invasion fleet, all but a dozen had been destroyed or run off.

But those dozen still made a hell out of the surface. And occasionally they directed a few missiles at the armored moon base to keep Chosinth and the others occupied.

"I'd enjoy bombing the snakes' planet," grumbled the pilot. "Slimy reptiles." He crossed himself again and found another saint to invoke when a new round of P'torra shelling rocked them. The only cheer Ralston found in the man's words was the weakness of his cursing against the Nex. The P'torra ferocity in destroying the planetary surface worked on the pilot's sympathy.

"How much longer before they finish all the repairs on the ship?" asked Ralston.

"If they finished four days ago, it wouldn't be soon enough for me." The pilot turned and studied a readout on the panel, then said, "I think they'll have most of the important work done within ten hours. I want to be out of here in eleven. You have Dr. Bernssen and the others ready for liftoff then. I don't care if anyone gets hurt or not, we're flaming out of here!"

"I'll warn them about your intentions," promised Ralston. He had much more on his mind. He had given Chosinth his word that everyone in the expedition would send preliminary drafts of their scientific papers to a Nex representative before publication. He had promised. Now he had to convince Bernssen to agree. And Westcott. And Leonore. And all the others.

Ralston made his way down the central passage and found Nels and Leonore in the large lounge area. They talked quietly and intensely. Ralston didn't want to disturb them but had no choice. Time pressed in on him and required immediate decisions.

Nels Bernssen looked up. He was obviously not pleased to be interrupted.

"Wait, Nels, please," said Ralston, cutting the other man off before he could protest. "I've got something important that's got to be said right now."

"How are the repairs coming?" Nels asked.

"Fine. We'll be shifting in eleven hours. I don't think the pilot wants to stay to even test the Nex equipment."

"Understandable," murmured Leonore.

"I haven't told you what I promised to get the work done. It involves you and the others."

Leonore's eyes went wide as she imagined the horrors perpetrated on Ralston—and that which would be visited on the rest of them by the non-human Nex.

"It's not all that bad, but it *is* galling."

"We won't turn over the chaos weapon to them," Bernssen flatly said. "We're agreed on that point. No one race gets it."

"Agreed," said Ralston. "I'm not sure I want even our people to have control of it." He heaved a deep breath, then plunged into the explanation. "So," he finished, "they want first peek at our work before it's published. They'd get it after publication. This just gives them a few weeks or maybe less head start on the P'torra."

"You agreed to this?"

"We needed the gyroscope and new rocket tubes. Without the one we don't star accurately and without the tubes we can't even get into position for a shift."

"I don't like it," said Nels.

"I don't, either. How could you ever agree to this, Michael?" asked Leonore.

"What other choice did I have? We can't buy the equipment from them at any price. Chosinth made it clear that Tosoll is on a war footing. The P'torra attacks show that the regent's not exaggerating the danger they face daily. And there's nowhere else to turn. We fell into their base. Without this agreement we'd be virtual prisoners until they decided to get rid of us."

Leonore shuddered at the way he'd worded it.

"They wouldn't kill us," Ralston said. "But the Nex have no incentive to let us go, either, unless I agreed. This isn't *that* bad."

"The precedent it sets is bad," said Bernssen.

"I know, I know. Can you think of any other way around this? We have to pursue the chaos device. If Westcott is right, it is falling apart even as we sit here."

"He might not be right," said Leonore. "He was wrong about the Beta primary and when it'd go nova."

"But he was right in how he used the chaos equations to get us through the middle of the P'torra fleet. Do you know anyone else who could have done that?" countered Ralston.

"It might have been luck—or stark insanity." Nels Bernssen slumped down, arms crossed tightly across his chest and his face clouded with emotion. He thought hard for a few minutes, then said, "The Nex don't have to see every paper. Yours and Leonore's will be innocuous enough. Even mine might be, since it deals with stellar mechanisms. Explaining how the fusion process proceeds is different from telling how to build a machine to disrupt it. There's always the chance we won't be publishing anything at all, that the trip will turn out different from what we expect.

"But Westcott," Nels went on. "He's another story. If we're successful, he'll be able to spell out in mathematical detail how the chaos equations can be used. The maneuvering he did would be a small part. He might be able to give ways of predicting how to topple a society or all the rest we've talked about. His papers will be important."

"Withholding them from the Nex isn't possible," said Ralston.

"Because you promised?"

"Because they know everyone aboard ship. And no, I didn't tell Chosinth. He already knew. The Nex have effective intelligence-gathering networks."

"Slenth had shown an interest in this expedition," finished Leonore. "Their communication network must be extraordinary for Chosinth to hear about us—and the chaos field—less than two months after we leave Novo Terra."

"We must continue," said Ralston. "We need to find the chaos device as quickly as possible. Whether Westcott is right in his calculations or the device will last a million years, we *must* find it."

"I agree," said Bernssen. "Better us than either the Nex or the P'torra."

"Do we keep silent after we've found it?" asked Leonore.

"Let's worry about that when we finish. Right now, do you agree to the Nex condition?"

"All right, Michael, I agree," said Leonore. "It really rankles. There should never be such conditions placed on research. It's not fair putting us under such pressure."

"They don't want to censor our findings, after all," said Ralston. "They just want a head start on the P'torra."

"They know better than to ask for us to hold back important details," said Bernssen. "We'd never agree. I'd hate to spend the rest of my life in remand, but I'd do it rather than give in to censorship or publishing false data. Better not to publish anything."

"What of Westcott?"

"His interests are so varied, there's no telling what he would want to publish. Remember how enthused he was about his quantum gravity theory? As far as I can tell," said Bernssen, "he's dropped all work on it in favor of the chaos equations solution. He might decide that the chaos device isn't important and go off on still another tangent."

"We've got to ask him."

"Let's get on our way, then worry about it," suggested Lenore.

Ralston didn't like this but his heart wasn't in confronting Westcott on the matter. What worried him the most was Chosinth's reaction to this cowardice on his part. The Nex regent had to know everything that went on inside the ship. Those probes attached to the hull were sensitive spy devices.

"I've got to ask him," Ralston decided. "Besides, we need a course to follow. We ended up at Tosoll by accident. Westcott must have a trajectory plotted by now."

Both Nels and Leonore nodded. They seemed restrained, possibly because of those Nex spy probes.

Ralston found Westcott hunched over the computer. He reached out to break the infrared beam but the mathematician's hand shot up to grab his wrist.

"That gives me a headache. I've told you that before. Do you want me to write it down for you so you won't forget?"

"Sorry, but we have a major problem."

"About the Nex demand to see our papers before publication? There is no dilemma involved. We must track the field. Therefore, any agreement allowing us to do so is in everyone's best interest."

"How'd you . . ." Ralston's question trailed off. Westcott was hooked into the computer and must have sophisticated sensing equipment of his own monitoring the Nex spy probes. After all, everything ran through the ship's computer—and in a sense because of his direct-link, Westcott *was* the ship's computer. Ralston held back a broad smile.

"Here. Take this to the pilot. It's a course input for the navigation computer." Westcott's watery eyes locked with Ralston's. The silent message was apparent: Do not allow the Nex access to the course information.

"I'll see that he gets it. How near completion are the repairs?"

"The gyroscope is installed and checks out. The one we built is more accurate. We should consider contacting the father of that assistant of yours—what's his name?"

"Leonid Disa?"

"He's the one. Interstellar Computronics can make a fortune off a precision instrument like this. We can get enough in royalties to finance a hundred new expeditions."

"What about the rockets?"

"Almost done. Testing them will be more difficult. Must blast for at least five minutes to burn off the protective layers of graphite and get down to the boron-fiber ceramic throats. Always dangerous since slightly less than two percent are defective. A tiny crack or chipped area means a blown rocket."

Ralston started to ask how Westcott had become such an authority, then stopped. The mathematician had full access to the ship's data banks. Such information had to be there for the pilot's benefit in any foreseeable emergency situation.

"Eleven hours?" asked Ralston. "Is that a good estimate for completion and launch?"

"I've done the calculations for such a time." Westcott turned away and hunched back toward the IR sensor on the computer console. Ralston took this as dismissal.

He left, almost cheerful again. Dealing with Westcott over the Nex demand had proven easier than he'd thought. Maybe the other rough spots would prove equally smooth once they came to them. Ralston hoped so, but he didn't believe it. The chaos device lay ahead somewhere in uncharted space—and he had seen how it had destroyed untold billions of people and two entire solar systems.

What other destruction did it hold in store for them? Ralston knew they'd find out soon.

"We are an escort for you until there is no more orbit," said the commander of the Nex military force.

"We won't need it," said the pilot. He crossed himself, then vanished toward the cockpit, not waiting to hear the answer.

"Are there still P'torra ships in orbit around Tosoll?" asked Ralston.

"Some. One," admitted the commander. "Regent Chosinth wants none of the wrong mistakes to be made. You are many valuables to us, he orders me."

"Damn right, we're valuable," grumbled one researcher. Ralston motioned him to silence. The scientist moved away to find an acceleration couch and strap down.

"We've given you our course heading," said Ralston, wondering how far off it really was. Probably not by much. Westcott had calculated it, possibly using the chaos equations to provide an added degree of randomness to the trip. They had all agreed that the Nex would be unable to follow, even knowing their precise heading. The length of their shift mattered as much as the heading, but Ralston had agreed that even this small bit of information should be hidden from the Nex, if possible.

Considering the Nex intelligence network and how efficiently it had operated so far, he doubted they hid much from the beady black serpents' eyes.

"Thank Chosinth for the hospitality. We won't forget it."

"He knows *you* will not forget, Dr. Ralston," said the military commander. The Nex turned and looked from Westcott to Bernssen and then to Leonore. His tongue flashed forth and quivered, then vanished between scaly lips. The Nex left quickly, motioning to his guard. In less than a minute, the reptiles had dropped to all fours and slithered from the research ship.

"I'm ready to blast," came the pilot's terse words over the

intercom. "Let's hope I catch a few of those snakes in the rocket wash."

Ralston hopped into a couch next to Nels. On the blond scientist's other side rested Leonore, her hand in his.

"We'll be all right," said Ralston. "But after we make the shift, we'll have to examine every part of the ship. I don't want to be carrying any recording equipment that's not ours."

"Do you think they'd do something that blatant?" asked Bernssen.

"Not really." Ralston settled into the couch when he felt vibrations from the rockets shake the entire ship. "But it can't hurt."

"We're off!" cried the pilot.

Ralston closed his eyes as the abrupt acceleration rammed him deep into the couch cushions. Nothing had gone right recently, but still he felt a curious hope warming him inside. Their deal with the Nex meant little. They would only receive information a bit ahead of the P'torra this way—and Ralston couldn't know in advance what that information might be.

This expedition might unleash a Pandora's box of nameless chaotic horror. Radioactive decay of once-stable elements. Mutation. Epilepsy. Devastating weather patterns. Stellar imbalances. Others that he couldn't even guess at.

But this hadn't happened yet. He screwed his eyes even tighter when a new fist of acceleration pounded at his chest. Whatever happened, he knew he couldn't go back on his word to Chosinth. Without personal honor, nothing mattered. Nothing.

"I got us lining up just fine," said the pilot. "We'll be shifting in about ten minutes. Everything's working great."

Ralston turned toward Westcott. He forced his eyelids open to see that the mathematician lay on his couch, sensor in a special brace so that the infrared beam wouldn't deviate from its receptor atop the computer console.

"What's the status, Westcott?" he called. The mathematician grunted against the force of their blast.

"Gyroscope is functional and on our star target. Tubes have burned through their protective layer. No cracks. No holes in the throat liner. We're going to shift without problem."

"Let the pilot do it," ordered Bernssen. "No need to upset him further."

"I . . . have computation to do before shift," said Westcott. "He is welcome to his ship."

Barely three minutes had passed before the pilot bellowed, "I'm picking up a radar trace. I think we have company. Mother of God, we do! It's one of those damned P'torra ships dogging us!"

Ralston fought to lift his hand to the intercom call button. He failed. He had to listen to the pilot without being able to respond.

". . . the snake ship's vectoring in to protect us. I didn't believe they'd risk their scaly skins to help us, but they are. St. Francis, yes, there they go!"

On the viewscreen Ralston saw tiny blips appear. The perspective distorted what actually happened in space. Even smaller blips began curving back and forth, some colliding, others slipping by: These were deadly missiles.

"The Nex got a hit in on the P'torra. Three minutes to our shift. Everything still functioning to optimal. Shift timer's on. We're going, no matter what."

"Westcott!" called Leonore. "Can you tell us what's going on out there?"

The mathematician grunted again. His voice came muffled and indistinct. "Want to work. No time for this. No time."

"Westcott!"

"The P'torra ship is not destroyed. It is launching all its missiles, hoping one will penetrate the Nex defenses."

"Are we behind the Nex ship?" asked Ralston. From the viewscreen he thought they might be in the direct line of fire if the Nex warship was destroyed. Another two minutes and it would no longer matter; they'd have starred out after the chaos device.

But until that instant, they were vulnerable.

"The Nex stopped all the missiles. No, wait, one penetrated its defenses."

Ralston didn't need Westcott to tell him that the Nex ship was in serious trouble. The sudden flare on the screen told of a hit. How serious he couldn't say. They'd need special radar to tell that. At these distances they watched the results of a battle that had occurred thirty seconds earlier. The speed of light was insufficient for learning the outcome.

"Westcott, is that a P'torra missile? Did one miss the Nex and come on after us?"

"The Nex ship is destroyed. It blew apart trying to protect us, according to my analysis of their maneuvers."

"Oh, my God, no!" cried Ralston. He had seen this happen before. The Nex made no provision for surrender on their warships. If this ship had been destroyed, it might have cast all its unspent missiles into space. Any differential motion each missile sensed would activate it and send it on its deadly mission.

The Nex warship itself might trigger a response; so would the P'torra ship. And so would the research ship.

"Four missiles abandoned, then launched spontaneously," came the pilot's voice. A quick prayer, then, "We've got twenty seconds until we star away from Tosoll."

"Westcott," asked Ralston, not wanting to know but having to ask. "How long before those missiles reach us?"

"Ten seconds," came the mathematician's answer. "Only ten seconds. We'll never have time to escape!"

Ralston gritted his teeth and began the death count.

Ten, nine, eight . . .

THIRTEEN

MICHAEL RALSTON FOUND himself unable to take his eyes off the viewscreen. The sight of the missiles coming for them—Nex missiles—hypnotized him.

". . . four, three . . ." He wished he could stop counting the seconds until their deaths.

The shift took him by surprise. At first he thought the sudden disorientation and sensory confusion he had come to experience at starring out and death were identical. He tasted the sounds and smelled the colors and screamed and saw the voiceless cry hang suspended before him. Ralston forced himself to relax. Slowly, the scrambled sensation loosened its grip in him and sounds became sounds, sights became sight.

"We did it!" he crowed when he was able. Ralston looked around the lounge area. Westcott still lay on his acceleration couch, head fastened down so that he wouldn't lose contact with the computer. Nels Bernssen had unfastened his restraining straps and held Leonore Disa tightly, rocking her back and forth as if she were a small child. The others in Bernssen's expedition moaned and moved slowly, barely understanding how they had escaped.

Ralston hit the call button and yelled at the pilot, "What happened? How did we avoid the missiles?"

"The Nex," the pilot mumbled. "By the saints, they gave their lives to protect us."

"What happened?" Ralston demanded a second time.

"They cast out their missiles to get the P'torra. Two of

them did. But one missile came for us because we were in motion. But, St. Jude be praised, we were accelerating too hard for it to catch us. We had enough of a start. We shifted just as it reached us."

"Is the ship all right?"

"Verd," said the pilot. "Everything shows green here. The missile might have exploded, but it couldn't touch us once we folded space around ourselves. Both St. Francises, thank you!"

The pilot started thanking a pantheon of saints. Ralston slumped and rested his head against the cool composite bulkhead of the ship. His feet rose and went over his head with the motion. They had, indeed, achieved stardrive. The weightlessness told of that.

Ralston heaved a deep breath, spun adroitly, and kicked over to where Westcott still lay unmoving. The infrared sensor blinked on and off slowly, showing most of Westcott's time was spent thinking rather than computing.

"The pilot says we made it. Did the shift come precisely on our target?"

"There is something wrong," said Westcott in a slow, almost drugged voice. "I cannot see what it is. There are strange attractors in this area that have never existed before."

"Strange attractors?"

"Mathematical points on an imaginary plot like nodes in real space. We seem to be lodged in one."

"We can't get out?" Ralston refused to feel panic. They had just escaped one of the most efficient and deadly weapons ever built. The Nex missiles seldom missed their targets and had destroyed one another. Luck had been a part of it, but they had survived.

Perhaps, reflected Ralston, luck mattered more when it came to survival than skill. The Alphans had been adroit, successful—and the chaos weapon had destroyed their culture, their population, their solar system. The Betans had been vastly more alien, but the passage of the chaos field had tainted them, also. Ralston screwed his eyes shut and tried to imagine the cleansing flame from the nova turning the monstrous gas giant planet into superheated vapor. What had the Betans done to deserve such a fate?

What had he and the others on this expedition done to deserve escape from death?

"It must be the result of the shift mathematics," said Westcott.

"What must?" Ralston came back to his senses and tried to pay more attention to what Westcott said.

"When we star out, all the distance is traveled in the first split second. The rest of the time is spent forcing our way back into space. The longer the shift, the harder it is to get free and the longer it takes."

Ralston blinked. He had never heard this. All the months he'd spent in space, he'd naively assumed that the distance was covered in some linear fashion, that every day's travel got them that much farther along toward their destination.

"If anything disturbs the shift space, we can find ourselves thrown out, not at the point we intended but at some other spot on a sphere with the same shift-distance radius."

"If we star for ten light years, you mean, and something disturbs us, we won't end up at the spot we intended but at another point on a ten light-year sphere?"

"It's more complex than that, but it's verd. We must be close to the chaos field. It has produced the attractor."

"What does this mean? We won't be able to leave shift space?" This frightened Ralston more than anything else about travel. To be forever doomed to weightlessness and the meaningless jumble shown on the viewscreen was a hell he wanted to avoid.

"I don't know what it means. The strange attractors are points of utter stability in a sea of chaos. This is the product of the equations' solution. What can it mean?"

Westcott closed his eyes and the dim red light on his head-mounted sensor began to glow constantly. Ralston pushed himself away to let the mathematician work through this problem.

It sounded as if they were trapped, but Westcott hadn't seemed concerned on this point. But the man had been worried. Ralston saw this. He forced himself to laugh ruefully. Westcott's concerns were not those of ordinary mortals. He might be worrying over an abstruse solution rather than their plight. If it could even be called that.

They were alive! In that Ralston rejoiced.

What did it mean to be in a well of stability during a shift?

"We will shift free and find what we want," said West-cott. The mathematician lounged back on the acceleration couch as if barely able to hold himself erect. In the weight-lessness of the ship, this made Westcott appear even more enervated.

"Is he all right?" asked Leonore, whispering to Ralston.

"I can't say. He hasn't eaten, he doesn't sleep, he just works."

"How can you tell?"

"The sensor has been glowing a brighter red than normal. I think he must be forcing hundreds of hours of work into just a few."

"I don't want to be caught in mid-shift," said Leonore. Her brown eyes welled with tears. Ralston thought that this expedition had been hard on her—and on Bernssen. They had left under the stigma of Ralston's problems at the University, had found mistakes in Westcott's calculations that robbed them of precious months of research, had fallen into the middle of a renewed Nex–P'torra conflict and now they had finally tracked the chaos device and found themselves caught in a spacial anomaly created by the chaos field's passage.

"We won't get lost. Westcott's assured me that won't happen." Ralston went on to explain how they might end up at some unknown point on an imaginary sphere with the radius of their shift, but that would be better than coming out of the shift in some distant galaxy, lost beyond all hope of return.

"I always knew starring was more of a mathematical con-cept than something definite," the woman said, "but I'd never realized it was that abstract."

"The attractor!" cried Westcott. His eyes blazed as brightly as the infrared sensor mounted on his shaved head. "We have reached the proper point."

Ralston cried in surprise when the ship lurched. He fell heavily, hitting his knees on the floor. It took Ralston several seconds to realize that they had regained gravity and that this was the source of his problems. He straightened painfully, rubbing his skinned knees and a banged elbow.

"Are we out of the shift?" he asked. Something deep within him told him that the danger—whatever it might be—wasn't past.

"Yes. No. I can't say where we are," said Westcott. "We have entered a new type of space, one with a physical reality different from what we've known."

"Physical laws still operate?" demanded Bernssen. "Space is still isotropic, isn't it?"

"I don't think so. We . . . it's difficult to say how this space operates. We have fallen into a special type of well. Not a gravity well. This isn't a topological quantity in the same sense that gravity is. It's *different*."

Ralston looked up at the viewscreen and thought that his eyes had been affected by the shift.

The silence that fell when the others looked made Ralston even more uncomfortable.

"Are those all starships?" Leonore asked, her voice cracking with strain. "It's as if they were sucked into this hole and . . ."

"And couldn't get out," finished Ralston.

Nels Bernssen began snapping orders. "I want a full scan of whatever's there. Entire spectrum. Photos. Find out if there's any hard radiation. Do it now!"

A dozen of the researchers jumped and ran down toward the cargo hold to unlimber their equipment.

"All different shapes and designs," said Ralston. "It's like an old Earth legend. What was it? I remember. The Sargasso Sea. Legend held that ships blundering in were trapped for all eternity."

"It's no illusion," came McGhee's voice from across the room. The scientist pressed himself close to a control panel he'd mounted on the bulkhead. Outside the ship ran his probes. "Solid."

"It's a treasure trove!" cried Leonore, coming out of her shock. "There must be a half-dozen different kinds of ships. And each is unlike anything I've ever seen."

"I agree," said Ralston. "Any one of those ships consti-

tutes a major find. If we can trace their origins back to a
home planet, we can be listed as discoverer.'' Ralston rocked
back and held down the bitterness that welled up within him.
''Dammit, listen to me. I'm starting to sound like Jaime
Velasquez. It's *knowledge* I should be thinking about, not
gain.''

Ralston's mind still lovingly cherished the idea of being the
primary discoverer of a new humanoid race. One percent of
any trade, any scientific exchange, any gain whatsoever from
that planet's society, went to the discoverer. One such find
made men wealthy beyond the dreams of avarice. Presented
for Ralston were a minimum of six different types of ship,
any one of which might be enough.

''Salazar would let you back into his good graces,'' said
Nels. ''Imagine being able to buy the entire University. You
could—we all could. Even splitting the take among us all,
each of us could buy a dozen Universities of Ilium.''

''As if we'd want it,'' said Leonore.

Ralston wasn't sure that this wasn't exactly what he wanted.

''We're missing something,'' he said. ''Those ships are
here because they couldn't get out. We might be trapped,
too.''

All eyes turned to Westcott. The mathematician sat with
glazed eyes. Spittle ran from the corner of his mouth. Seldom
had Ralston seen a man so oblivious to the world around him.
Or was Westcott more aware than any of them? The sensor
glowed brilliantly now. Whatever the man worked on, it had
to be of solid, significant importance to them all.

''Westcott? What is it?'' asked Nels. The physicist shook
the mathematician's shoulder slightly. ''What readings are
you getting from the ship's external sensors?''

''We are the only life in the attractor pocket,'' Westcott
said. ''Dead ships. All are dead ships—and all failed in
precisely the same manner. This spot draws a particular
dysfunction.''

''Did it cause the problem?'' asked Ralston.

''No, not at all. Those ships. All have a stardrive signifi-
cantly different from ours. The mathematics of their operation
is not ours. The chaos field passed by, disrupted their spacial
manifold, and jerked the ships to this stability point.''

"We're in no danger, are we?" asked Leonore.

"Our drive was interrupted, not destroyed as theirs was. We . . . we can continue on our course in a few hours. We must build up speed again, as if we were accelerating to a shift. But it'll seem that we're stationary. This is not the space we came from, nor is it the space we normally occupy during a shift."

"If he says we're in good shape, I'll believe him," said Leonore. The woman's face glowed with excitement. "We've got a chance to do some archaeology, Michael. Do you want to go with me?"

"Which one?" asked Ralston. His heart beat faster. The idea of discovering not one race, but six thrilled him. He had been cheated out of full research on the Alphans and the Betans, but not now. He'd find these aliens' star charts and track them down. If they still lived and prospered, fine. If only ruins remained, he'd have a lifetime of work ahead of him picking and choosing the best sites to explore and reconstruct.

"The nearest one. We can work across from it. I'll want a supervisor, ten—no, make that twenty!—probes, enough block circuits to record everything a dozen times over."

Leonore's enthusiasm for the unexpected find was contagious. The others in Bernssen's expedition began chiming in with their findings. No hard radiation. No reason for the gravity field; it was simply there. Fourteen ships within observation range, only two of them with similar design. Measurements were being made at a frantic pace.

Ralston and Leonore walked quickly to the airlock, gathering their equipment as they went, arguing over the best way of examining their lucky find.

"Nothing but probes first," insisted Ralston. "We'll want a gas-content probe, all the visual spectrum on another, hard UV and IR on another, one to drill for samples of the hull, at least five for any bodies we find."

"We can go in ourselves," said Leonore, "and save a lot of time."

"Too dangerous," said Ralston. "We're expecting to find no one alive. How do we know they're not all waiting for us?"

"Better and better."

"They might have died from something not inherent in this." Ralston gestured vaguely, indicating the attractor well.

"Westcott said this is only a mathematical concept. How can that kill anyone?"

"How can it hold so many ships? And we'll want a couple probes to begin work on dismantling their drive system. If it's different, we'll want to know how."

"That's low priority, Michael."

"High priority," he contradicted. "We're still looking for the chaos device, remember? We need all the data we can for Westcott to determine how it affected the drives. Might give him a clue to the workings of the chaos device."

"Well, all right," Leonore agreed reluctantly. "We certainly need a probe for photographing their charts and for worming around in their computer. And their communications gear. We need—"

"Everything," Ralston cut in, laughing. He felt the same ebullience. So much to do and so little time to do it. He sobered when he considered how little time they might have. Lingering in this anomaly wasn't much to his liking, even if it did present such a wide variety of fascinating discoveries.

"Can we send at least one probe to each of the other ships within range?" he asked.

"There's no need. We can go through the others one by one, when we finish with the first." Leonore started to say something more, then clamped her mouth shut and looked like a fish out of water. "We can't examine them all, can we? We'll have to leave sometime. Nels and the others will want to get on."

"The chaos device. That's what we're all agreed on finding." Too many times interesting but tangential topics presented themselves. It took real discipline to let those avenues pass by untouched while pursuing the main topic. If this rule wasn't strictly adhered to, nothing would ever get done.

"It's not fair," grumbled Leonore. "How do we mark this spot in space so we can come back—or at least give the coordinates to another researcher?"

"I don't know. We'll have to ask either Westcott or the pilot and find out." Ralston didn't want to consider the chance that they'd never be able to return, that this trip had been caused by the chaos field and duplicating its random effect would be impossible.

"Where are you two going?" came Bernssen's stern voice as they were suiting up for the trip to the nearest of the alien vessels. "You can't personally go to one of those ships."

"Why not?"

"We're getting ready to leave. Westcott says it's now or never."

"No!" protested Ralston. "We need the information locked in those ships. We do! We need to find out how they failed so that Westcott can prevent the same thing from happening to us when we get to the chaos device."

Bernssen shuffled his feet, then shook his head. "I'm primary researcher on the expedition, Michael. I'm in charge. I can't let you go—either of you."

"How long?" demanded Ralston. "Long enough to send over a few probes?"

"You'll probably lose them."

"Send them. Now!" snapped Ralston. Softer, he said, "Sorry, I'm used to being in charge."

"You're not in charge," Leonore reminded him. "If Nels says we might lose the probes, we've got to consider if it's worth saving them for later." She smiled wickedly.

As one, she and Ralston said, "Launch the probes!"

"I'd help," said Bernssen, "but I've got to keep a close watch on my own monitoring equipment. Make it quick and don't interfere with any of my readings."

"How long do we have?" asked Ralston, already programming the supervisor to handle ten probes, each capable of measuring and sending back different data.

"Less than you need. So hurry."

Ralston and Leonore were sweat-soaked by the time they finished their programming. The master computer controlled the probes perfectly; the ten small, silver fish-shaped probes darted across the short distance to the nearest ship.

"Definitely alien design," said Ralston, checking the visual readouts. "I've got photos of the exterior hull and the equipment hanging on it. Going around to the stern. You search for their airlock and try to get in that way. I may try burrowing through their hull to record the composition."

"That's dangerous, Michael, especially if any of them are still alive."

"Do you think any of them are?"

"We go in through the airlock or not at all," Leonore decided.

Ralston wanted information, not safety, but he acquiesced. Leonore Disa was, after all, in command. He had agreed to this before leaving Novo Terra, and he wasn't going back on his word. He had ceased being the instructor and was now the associate of a former student.

"No rocket nozzles," he said. "Wonder how they maneuver when they're not under stardrive?" The supervisor began to hum as its block circuits recorded everything sent back by the ten probes.

"Got it!" cried Leonore. "Their airlock. But I don't see the activator mechanism."

"There. There it is. But there's no power on it." Ralston bounced the probe off what he thought was the opening mechanism and finally gave up. "This might be a mechanical assist," he said. Ralston guided one probe in against a large, circular plate in the center of the door, applied the probe's magnetic snout, had some difficulty in getting it to grip, found a hold, then used side jets to rotate the probe. The rotary motion spun the plate and the airlock slid open soundlessly.

"Can't keep all the probes going manually," said Leonore. "Put three on automatic and let them scour the ship's outer hull. The others we put inside. You take four, I'll take three. You go for the engines. I'll find the cockpit."

Sweat poured into Ralston's eyes as he worked his four probes back through the winding maze of the alien starship's corridors. Using the infrared did little to aid him. The interior of the ship had long since cooled to a point where everything had come to thermal equilibrium. Cursing, Ralston took a chance. He reached across Leonore and flipped a switch.

"Michael, stop! You're going to destroy a probe!"

"Going to blow it apart to give some heat. I need to see where I'm going."

"Not much in the spectrum, is there?" she admitted. "We should have outfitted one probe with a headlamp."

"Didn't think it'd be needed. My fault. I'm used to exploring warmer ruins, though."

"I'm in charge. It's my oversight."

"There!" cried Ralston. The probe exploded nicely and sent heat radiating down the long corridor. The afterglow where it warmed the walls allowed Ralston to drive forward quickly and find the engine compartment. One probe he set to burrowing. The other two he put on automatic, but he quickly ran into the same problem. The heat from the destroyed probe had not penetrated the engine room.

"Got a couple bodies," said Leonore. "Can't think what else they'd be."

"Any power sources at all?"

"Nothing. No radioactivity, nothing."

"Here goes another probe," he said, flipping the toggle that sent the destruct message through the supervisor to the probe. The remaining two probes processed information at a furious clip.

But it wasn't fast enough.

"We're getting up to speed," came Bernssen's words from the cargo hold. "Westcott says it's now or never. The entire attractor is sucking up our energy and driving everything to zero point. Radioactivity, our power plant, our bodies, everything. If we don't start now, we're going to be sapped and trapped."

"Sapped and trapped?" exploded Leonore. "Did you come up with that on your own?"

"Westcott's words," Nels said almost sheepishly. "But they fit. A couple reports of batteries being drained have already come in. Equipment's failing, as a result. We've got to leave."

"Just a few more minutes," begged Ralston.

"Now. It's now or never."

Ralston looked over to the supervisor's panel. It took in prodigious amounts of information from his two working probes and the three Leonore had roaming the starship's cockpit, but it wasn't enough. Not by days, months, perhaps years, was it enough.

Robbed again. Michael Ralston once more had a career-making discovery ripped from his grasp.

The research ship shuddered and strained, as if it were chained down. They had begun their flight back into normal space.

FOURTEEN

"WE NEED MORE time!" cried Michael Ralston. "We can't leave yet. Please!"

Even as he spoke the research ship shuddered harder, struggling against unseen bonds.

"Give it up, Michael," said Leonore Disa. "The probes are dead. We don't seem to have moved a micron, yet the indicators show we've gone beyond their effective transmission range."

Ralston worked at the supervisor's console for several minutes before coming to the same conclusion. The ship had somehow gone beyond the considerable transmission range of their probes, yet visually the alien derelict lay exactly where it had before. The laws of physics in the attractor well had been redefined in ways Ralston couldn't begin to comprehend.

"All our equipment has gone dead, too," said Nels Bernssen. The blond physicist stood with his arm around Leonore's shoulders. "It's best we get out of this spacial backwater as quickly as possible. It's draining all our stored energy."

Ralston sat down heavily, disconsolate. He shivered, wrapped his arms around himself, and asked peevishly, "Is that why it's getting so cold in here?"

"Ship's temperature hasn't changed but a degree or so. It's you, Michael," said Nels. "The attractor is sucking away your vitality." Bernssen rubbed one hand up and down his arm. "It's working that way on us all. There's a leveling or neutralizing process at work I don't begin to understand.

151

Nothing but gravity—the weakest of the forces, oddly enough—seems to have survived by the way the ships cluster together. Barranquilla was working on magnetic moment measurement of the ship, and she found it to be decreasing rapidly. Almost nothing of a magnetic nature can last longer than a week inside this field. Electrical is going at a measurable rate."

"A vampire sucking its prey," muttered Ralston.

"What's a vampire?" asked Bernssen.

"Are we getting free?" asked Ralston. "Freezing to death isn't too cheerful a prospect."

"We might not even freeze," said Nels. "Chances looked good that our bodies would simply stop converting food into energy for us. That's the least efficient of any of the chemical processes."

"But to leave it all. We needed more time. We hardly have one block circuit of information about that alien ship. I'm not sure we can figure out how its engines worked, either. The two probes had only begun scanning the control equipment."

"One probe of mine scanned what may be the aliens' star charts. We'll have to analyze the data to see."

"That's something, but not too much. I wanted to give Westcott the complete design of the alien stardrive so he could determine how this attractor worked."

"It must be an important part of the chaos field's effect," said Nels Bernssen. "Everything works in reverse here due to the chaos induced by the device."

"What do you mean?" asked Leonore.

"The field causes random events to happen, creating its own cause and effect relationship in real space. But here, just the reverse occurs. Everything smooths out, falls into one energy level. In a way, what the attractor holds is the ultimate fate of the universe. Entropy has increased to the point where everything is homogeneous. This is the exact opposite of chaos. This is sameness. Forever."

"The ships hadn't fallen apart," said Ralston. "That means the binding forces holding the metallic lattices together hadn't given up and turned into soup."

"In time," said Bernssen. "That's my first guess, at least. Any idea how long those ships had been inside?"

Ralston shook his head. They had nothing to use as a

measure. If they'd found a radioactive material aboard, this might have given some clue. Or perhaps not, if what Bernssen said was true. The radioactive isotopes might have decayed far faster than their "natural" half-lives demanded.

"The alien bodies were in good condition," said Leonore. "No decomposition that I saw."

"What's to decay the bodies?" asked Nels. "All the microbes likely to cause the decomposition are dead, too. Only the dissolving of the electronic bonds in the bodies themselves would cause the flesh to fall off the bones."

"We—" Ralston stood and took a step toward Leonore. The abrupt cessation of gravity sent him cartwheeling through the air, to smash hard against a bulkhead. He tried to grab a conveniently located elastic band and missed; he rebounded and sailed back into the room. Nels had been luckier. He and Leonore still stood with their arms around one another. Inertia held them for the brief instant it took for their space instincts to return and allow them to react by grabbing at the supervisor for anchoring.

"What happened?" cried Ralston, still struggling to control his spin. He hit the far bulkhead and succeeded in tangling one foot in an elastic band. Slamming hard against the wall produced a few bruises but he stopped his uncontrolled trip.

"We made it!" cried Nels Bernssen. "We shifted out of the attractor well!"

Ralston worried that they might have blundered into worse trouble. He had experienced none of the phenomena he'd come to associate with beginning a shift. He worked his way around, then kicked accurately and caught the edge of the supervisor on his way across the room. With deft movements, Ralston secured the computer equipment and vented a deep sigh at the lost probes. He could only hope that they had found something of interest before destruction.

Leonore popped the block circuit from the side of the supervisor and tucked it away in a special carrying case.

"For Westcott," she said.

"I want to talk with him to see what our progress is," said Ralston. Together, the three made their way up the central shaft and to the lounge where Westcott remained motionless, unchanged from when they'd last seen him. If Westcott's narrow chest wasn't rising and falling slowly, Ralston might have pronounced him dead. As it was, Ralston merely considered him not alive.

"The pilot needs someone to talk with," said Westcott. "He is frantic. I have control of the ship and cannot relinquish it for some time yet. Perhaps another hour."

"What happens then?" asked Ralston.

"We return to normal space."

"How's this possible? We can't be anywhere near ready to exit. We just began the shift." Ralston rubbed the bruised spots that gave mute testimony to how suddenly the shift had started.

"The strange attractor is a product of the chaos field. We were pulled along behind the field by the attractor. Yet we remained where we were, stationary in space."

"You're talking riddles."

"All this is one giant puzzle," said Westcott. "The mathematics are complex and not amenable to simple words." Westcott ran a pallid hand across his sweaty forehead. "They might not be amenable to even the force of my intellect. The chaos equations hold even more suprises than I'd thought at first."

"When we come out, will we be close to the device?"

"There is no other conclusion," said the mathematician. "The attractors are formed by the passage of the field. A symmetry *does* exist in the universe."

"How can there be symmetry," asked Bernssen, "when the chaos field is spreading randomness?"

Westcott chuckled. "The dice play God with the universe."

"We have the data from the alien ship," spoke up Leonore, not wanting to get into a theological argument with a mathematician. "You said the other ships used a different form of stardrive, one that quit when it came into contact with the chaos device's sphere of influence. Michael thinks a schematic of their engines might help you in working on a new solution to the chaos equations."

"It might, it might. If I can determine why their engines failed, it gives new perspective on how the chaos field interacts with and destroys classical mechanisms."

Westcott took the block circuit and slipped it into the side of the ship's computer. Westcott stiffened as the thundering assault of information flooded his brain and turned him into more of a computer than a human being. Settling back, he began forming theories and testing them mathematically.

"He's lost to us for a while," said Ralston. "I'll go calm the pilot."

"I . . . I'm tired," said Leonore, looking over at Nels. "I think I'll go to my cabin and get some rest."

"Remember what Westcott said. We come out of the shift in about an hour. Be sure you're strapped in for it," warned Ralston.

"We will be." Together Leonore and Nels floated away. Their soft voices vanished in the low-pressure bubble around them. Ralston closed his eyes for a moment, envying them. He'd been in love like that once, a long time ago. Old warmths rose within, along with the memories. Ralston pushed it all away, forced it down into the depths of his soul once again. There wasn't time for nostalgia—or was it better described as reveling in maudlin emotions?

He made his way to the cockpit where the pilot lit one votive candle after another on the small altar he had at the side of the controls. A small circulating fan kept the combustive gases from snuffing out the flames.

"Isn't it dangerous having all that open flame?" asked Ralston. "One good oxygen leak and you'd be fried."

"The saints won't permit it," said the man. "With all that's happened on this trip, I need to know that someone's listening to me. If not the saints, then who?"

He crossed himself and swung in a quick movement that deposited him directly in his command chair. Legs curled around the stanchions under it, the pilot seemed to be sitting down with the pull of gravity working on him.

"Has Westcott told you that we'll be reentering normal space in less than an hour?"

"That chinging son of a bitch has told me nada of what he does to my ship!" the pilot almost shouted. "*I* command this ship. I, Juan Jose Gonzales y Vega!"

Ralston blinked in surprise. Pilots normally kept to themselves and never had he heard a pilot reveal his name to a passenger. The pilots had their own superstitions and mores. Consorting with passengers seldom occurred because of the need for concentration when on duty—or so they claimed. Had Gonzales snapped under the extreme pressure of their expedition?

"Why don't you go to your quarters and relax? Take a short nap."

"Take drugs to calm me?" snapped Gonzales. "Pilots do not drug themselves under any circumstances. Never have I heard of a pilot taking even a painkiller!"

"The beta endorphins are natural painkillers," said Ralston before he realized that the pilot only raged because of Westcott assuming control of the starship.

"Look," said Ralston, trying to calm the man. "We're in grave danger because of our choice of investigation topics. The chaos field we pursue does things to people, to machines, even to stars."

"One of the physicists—the cute one with the nice ass—"

"Barranquilla," supplied Ralston, without even thinking.

"Verd, Dr. Barranquilla mentioned this to me that the chaos weapon reset the Beta star's inner mechanisms and caused it to go nova."

"There's much more. It can affect people by changing chemicals and electrical potentials in the brain. Epilepsy, even mutation, is a possible result of contact with the field."

Gonzales snorted in contempt at that. "I take all the precautions against radiation."

"This is a different type of radiation. It might even be different, not a radiation at all. Westcott calls it a concept rather than a physical reality, but it *does* interact with stars and biological organisms and most everything else."

"What do you tell me, Dr. Ralston?"

"Burn a few more candles for me. Implore the saints for help. But let Westcott run the ship for a little longer. He's the only one among us who can begin to understand what we're up against."

"Such is the nature of research, verd?"

"Verd," Ralston agreed.

"But it is accepted that *I* am pilot and in command? If a situation occurs where we are all in danger, I must act as pilot."

Ralston said nothing. He slapped the pilot on the shoulder and knew instantly that this was a mistake. Gonzales flinched back, not wanting any physical contact with his passenger. Ralston left the cockpit with its burning candles and upset pilot, knowing that the pilot didn't understand the magnitude of the chaos field's importance.

Michael Ralston wasn't sure that he understood.

The shift into normal space came with a jolt. Ralston strained against the straps on the couch and then sagged down, forcing his tensed muscles to relax. Across from him Westcott's eyelids fluttered and the mathematician came out of his trance.

"The pilot can have control back," said Westcott. "We have starred to a point within twenty light minutes of the chaos field."

"What?"

Ralston surged against the straps in an attempt to lift his head enough to see the viewscreen. Nothing appeared on it other than a star pattern similar to hundreds of others he'd seen over the years he'd spent in space.

"You cannot see it yet on the viewscreen," said Westcott. "It is a small planetoid, hardly two kilometers in diameter." The man shook his head slowly, the silver sensor mounted atop his bald pate gleaming brightly as his head turned. "Such a small device to bring such havoc to the universe."

"We'll get to monitoring it right away," said Ralston. He pulled the straps away from his body and swung out of the couch, kicking hard enough to send himself down the central shaft toward the cargo bay where much of their equipment had been set up.

Leonore and Nels already worked on a variety of instruments.

"Nels wanted to start the spectrographic photos right away," said Leonore, almost apologetically. "And I wanted to see if I could get another set of probes ready to go."

"Let me help." Ralston began working with Leonore, but soon stopped and stared at the cases. "These don't seem to respond when I press their test circuits. See?"

"Some of my equipment is malfunctioning, too," spoke up

Bernssen. "We're near the chaos weapon. We can't expect to have everything one hundred percent from now on."

Ralston swallowed hard. He had been touched by the chaos field's residual effects back in the Beta system. Using the telepathic projector left by the Alphans to learn about the travails in reaching Beta 5, he had shared the epileptic condition with the avian scientist making the recording. Ralston didn't remember the seizure, but the others had told him about it.

He had been touched by chaos. He felt an itching sensation up and down his spine and fear rose to the point where he wondered if he could contain it. Being this close to the source of so much chaotic misery might trigger a new and more dangerous seizure.

"It might not, Michael. We don't know enough," said Leonore, as if she'd read his mind.

"Am I that easy to read?" he asked.

"What else could you be thinking about?" she asked. Leonore rested her hand on his arm to reassure him. It helped, but not too much.

"Let's try to fix what we can in the probes. We'll want as many going out as possible when we get within range."

"Damn," complained Bernssen. "The block circuit for the spectrometer's gone haywire. Everything is beginning to fall apart randomly."

"Better have the automatic sedate everyone," Ralston suggested. "That helped back on Beta 5 to keep down the incidence of severe epileptic seizures."

"All right," said Bernssen. "I'll order it. But you're going first."

Ralston had no argument with that. They left Leonore to work on the equipment while they both returned to the lounge area. There, Ralston saw almost half of the expedition working on equipment mounted around the walls. He couldn't help but notice Barranquilla. The pilot was right. She did have a nice ass.

"What is it?" she asked, glancing back over her shoulder at Ralston. "Can I do something for you, Dr. Ralston?"

"Maybe later. Any trouble with your equipment?"

"None," the physicist said. "The computer failed to record properly while we were trapped inside the attractor, but now I'm getting strong magnetic moment measurement from the chaos field.'' Barranquilla sounded happy at the randomness flowing all around, but then she hadn't experienced its effects personally. She had readings now and, because of that, she was content.

"Everyone, listen up," called Bernssen. "Light sedation is required. We found it worked to lessen the chaos field's effect when we were exploring the ruins left on Beta 5."

"Those were residual effects," said a scientist. "We're dealing with primary sources now. I don't want to go around groggy because you've got me drugged to the ears. I'd prefer to take my chances."

"Everyone," insisted Bernssen. "This isn't open to debate. The auto-doc will be set for the lightest dosage possible. Ralston and I will go first, then the rest of you will let it inject you. I'll be back in an hour. I expect the auto-doc to register administering a dose to each of you. No exceptions."

Ralston rubbed his arm after the vapor injection from the automedic. It had broken blood vessels just under the skin, something that happened only with poorly calibrated automedics.

"We'd better run a check on its block circuit," said Ralston. "It's no more immune to the chaos field than we are."

"Good point. In fact," Nels said, "we'd better swoop in, collect our data, then get the hell away." He slammed a fist against the call button and roused the pilot from his work. "We want a hyperbolic trajectory past the planetoid. Navigate so that we'll spend a minimum of time within ten light seconds."

"That'll require hard acceleration."

"Do it. We've got our equipment lashed down."

"No close-in approach, no exploration, nothing? You come all this way and do nothing? What's with you people?"

"Do it," said Bernssen. He released the call button and turned to Ralston. "I think our pilot's not going to be able to stand the strain. It might be the chaos effects or it might just be losing control to Westcott."

At the mention of the mathematician, Ralston rotated slowly and faced the man. Westcott's eyes were open but unfocused.

A thin hand lifted and motioned to Bernssen and Ralston. The two swam over.

"The pilot's course is adequate. You've chosen well on course and duration. But I must be fully connected to the computer for maximum efficiency. The sedative you've ordered for the others will dull my senses and slow interfacing."

"I ordered everyone to get the sedative," said Bernssen. "It's for everyone's safety."

"It will prevent me from functioning to the fullest." Westcott sounded adamant about not taking the drug.

Ralston saw that the expedition leader wrestled with this problem. Allowing Westcott to avoid taking the calming drug could only cause dissension among those others who resented being sedated. What the mathematician said made sense. Speed of interaction with the computer was slowed by drugs.

"No sedative," Nels Bernssen decided. "But the automedic stays beside you. The first sign of trouble and it goes into action. And then it'll be everything, sedatives, whatever."

Westcott dismissed them with the wave of a hand, just as a Spanish king might have dismissed peasants from his court.

Leonore Disa returned to the lounge, eyes bright with anticipation. "Every probe we have is ready for launch. The supervisors will handle them."

"How many probes did you get working?" asked Ralston.

"Fifteen. Not as many as I'd've liked, but it should be enough." Leonore reached out when the ship vibrated. The rockets had cut in, positioning the research ship for its rapid hyperbola down and past the chaos device—and away.

"Here we go!" cried Ralston. The acceleration brought them to the floor of the lounge. He swung around and watched as Bernssen's researchers began flipping switches. All the equipment went to automatic. Nothing would be done manually; there wouldn't be time.

"He looks terrible," Leonore said. "Westcott. Look at him. I've seen corpses that looked healthier."

Ralston swallowed hard when he saw the gaunt, pallid face begin to contort as if in intense pain. Westcott screamed then and thrashed about. When his silver, shiny sensor lost line-of-sight contact with the infrared receptor mounted on the computer console, Ralston knew something had gone wrong.

"He's having a seizure. A big one, too," Ralston called. "Help me with him."

Westcott had been strapped down securely, but this hadn't saved him from injury. His powerful muscle contractions had broken one strap and left behind a bloody streak on the mathematician's thrashing legs. Ralston grabbed the auto-doc's probe and thrust it against Westcott's arm. Sedatives sprayed out and into the man's bloodstream but did little to quiet him.

"He's still linked to the computer," cried Leonore. "See? How's that affecting him?"

The sensor on Westcott's head gleamed as if it connected to the ship's computer. But they blocked it. It was as if Westcott had linked himself with a bigger machine, one vastly more potent—and couldn't handle the input.

"The chaos device's got him!"

Westcott jerked even harder, completely out of control, dominated by the enforced randomness of the chaos field.

FIFTEEN

MICHAEL RALSTON'S ARMS twitched and a curious sensation of falling came over him. The research ship accelerated and drove at the chaos device with such speed that the pull inside amounted to more than Novo Terra's gravity. Why should he feel as if he fell?

"The chaos field is affecting me, too," Ralston said to reassure himself that he hadn't gone insane. "Everything seems so strange." He blinked and saw a rainbow of colors. The whine from the rocket engines almost deafened him, and the heavy odor of ozone clung so tenaciously to the air that even the hard-working circulating fans and filters couldn't remove it.

Ralston sat down heavily at the edge of one couch and tried to control his fear. This was unlike the shift that hurled the ship to the stars. No sensory scrambling occurred now. Every sense reported accurately—but why did the colors still paint his vision like an artist's drop cloth? That came from somewhere.

It had to be induced by the chaos device.

"Michael, please. Help us with Westcott." Leonore's voice cut through the heavy fog of his thoughts. With some reluctance, he turned back to the mathematician. Westcott's condition hadn't changed, nor had it worsened.

"If the chaos field is holding him, only getting away from it will help. Where are we on the trajectory?"

Nels Bernssen moved heavily to a wall-mounted radar-ranging unit his team had installed. "We're less than a hundred thousand kilometers from the planetoid's surface. Most of the instruments seem to be functional and reporting accurately. We'll be swinging away from the device in another few seconds."

Even as he spoke, the ship shuddered and the acceleration vector changed, violently throwing them to the floor. Ralston got to hands and knees. One restraining strap across Westcott's chest had held the mathematician into his couch. Some of the others hadn't fared as well. Barranquilla moaned, her arm dangling at a crazy angle from being banged against the edge of her couch. McGhee wheezed noisily, as if he might have a punctured lung. A half-dozen others appeared in better shape. Of those in the cargo hold, Ralston had no clue about their condition. Ralston crawled to the automedic and punched in the command to do triage, then begin work patching up the researchers.

The machine whirred happily and set about its task. For long minutes it stood next to Westcott. Ralston finally hit the cancel command on it and sent the auto-doc on its rounds. Determining what had gone wrong in the mathematician's head would require facilities far beyond those available to a portable medical unit.

"You're so pale, Michael. If you're all right, can you help us check the equipment?" Leonore Disa bent over him. Ralston hadn't even realized that he still sat on the edge of the acceleration couch, staring at a blank bulkhead. He slowly nodded, wondering if his head would tumble from his shoulders. When this didn't happen, he decided that he might really survive.

"Come on." Leonore put an arm around his shoulders and helped him stand. The acceleration still pulled heavily at him, but he found himself enjoying its feel more than he'd have thought possible. Floating weightless for weeks and months took its toll on him, not just physically but mentally. He was a planet born and bred creature and he needed the reassurance of gravity's pull.

"You did well setting the automedic," said Nels. "McGhee was in bad shape. Hit the side of his head. Looks like it might be hemorrhage in the brain."

Ralston went to the auto-doc and tapped the keys on its report screen. "Code 2-23. That's, let me look it up, that's a subdermal hematoma. Guess you were right. He'll be the first one the automedic tends to when it's finished looking at the others."

"No one is dead," said Bernssen without any indication of triumph at this. "Let's see how the recording went."

They made a quick circuit around the lounge area and studied the readings on Bernssen's equipment. Half had failed. The other half had performed well. Going down to the cargo hold where the bulk of their equipment had been set up showed similar results.

"We have enough data to keep us busy for a dozen years," said Bernssen, satisfaction finally showing in face and tone. "The price wasn't too bad, either. McGhee's the worst injured. We can always get more equipment, especially after this trip."

"Westcott is badly hurt," said Ralston. "There may not be any way out of that coma for him. Not unless we can figure out the chaos device's true nature."

"Why do you say that?" asked Nels. "That damned direct-link he uses malfunctioned and that's what put him into the trance. The auto-doc can snap him out of it."

"No," said Ralston. "I have a gut-level feeling it's more complicated than that. You know how I get my senses mixed up at the beginning of a shift?"

"You're the only one I ever heard of who had that problem. Me, I just get a headache," said Nels.

"As we passed by the chaos device—at perigee—everything around me seemed more intense, more vibrant, more colorful. But there wasn't any sensory confusion. I saw and heard and smelled a thousand times better than I ever had."

Leonore wrinkled her nose. "You most certainly *don't* smell better than you ever did. The chemical showers make us all smell like dead goats."

"You know what I mean. I came alive, truly alive. It was the reverse of entering a shift."

"You thrive on chaos?" asked Nels.

"Maybe, in a way. Maybe the touch I got before has attuned me to it. We've got to get to work to see what data we've collected. There might be a clue in it that'll help both Westcott and me.'' Ralston turned to the supervisor. Of the fifteen probes sent out, only two had penetrated to the surface of the chaos planetoid. But these had sent back such a wealth of data that it stunned Ralston with the implications.

"It's all here," he said softly. "Look, Leonore, look. Markings on the lava upjuts. Those have to be writing. Instructions for operation? Warnings?"

"It might be a stellar return address. Sort of a 'if lost, return, compensation guaranteed.' "

"We'll need the ship's computer for detailed analysis," said Ralston. Adrenaline flowed through his body now. He had data to work with. They had found the chaos device and had accumulated much of what they sought. Now came the long, laborious—and, for Ralston, exciting—process of sifting through it and puzzling together the pieces to learn all they could about those beings who had built the device.

"We got good readings, too," said Bernssen, after checking with several others of his expedition in the cargo bay. "It might even be possible to analyze the field generation itself. We have enough different readings to give good guesses now. Somehow, all those have to correlate. With it, we can fit it into the way the field functions, why it seems to disrupt the laws of physics." Bernssen's eyes glowed. "We can even find out what initiates the instability that causes novas. When we do that, we'll have a better idea what causes natural ones. This is the find of a lifetime."

"No one's ever discovered anything like it, Nels," said Ralston. "In physics, in mathematics, in archaeology, we're all winners because of that thing."

Ralston's left arm twitched seriously, causing him to knock over a block circuit he'd set on top of the supervisor. Only Leonore's quick reflexes saved it before it hit the floor. Although such a fall wouldn't have damaged it, they were all tensed and acutely aware of anything out of the ordinary. Ralston grabbed his left arm with his right hand and held it down. The jerking ceased, but he felt sweat soaking his body.

"Would more sedative help?" asked Leonore, worried about him.

"Much more and I might pass out. There's too much to do for me to take a nap now."

The pilot interrupted them. "Do you want me to shut down the rockets or keep going? I'm getting indications of system failure throughout the ship. I need to tend to this before we shift."

"No shift," said Bernssen, hitting the call button. "We need to set up an orbit around the planetoid and continue surveillance."

"Orbit it? I'm not a genius like Westcott. I can't see how to do that. The godforsaken rock is accelerating and decelerating, although I don't see any rocket exhaust. I'd recommend just trying to parallel its course and watching carefully. I read us as being about eighty light seconds away from it."

"Maintain a parallel course at one hundred seconds," decided Bernssen. "And report immediately any major system failure."

"I'll do that," Gonzales said. "You can count on me doing that—and no closer." The pilot clicked off. Only irritating static remained on the intercom.

"We might be unable to do more than limp away from the planetoid, if we sustained too much chaotic damage," said Bernssen. "But it seems that we're in good enough shape to keep going for a while longer."

The uncontrollable twitching in his arm abated, and Ralston settled in to analyzing the prodigious amounts of data collected during their frenzied fly-by of the chaos planetoid. Ralston was fascinated by the rock spires and the obviously crafted caves visible in many of the probe photos. None of the probes had penetrated into those caverns, but Ralston thought they held the real chaotic secrets. In those dark holes lay the controls to the chaos device, its programming, its generating mechanism, everything about it that he wanted to know.

And behind the controls lay the intelligence that had formed them. What of the builders? Ralston hoped for photos of the creators but knew that wasn't likely. If this had been built as a weapon, those building it weren't likely to send photos. But it didn't have to be a weapon. It might be another race's attempt to contact others. If they were truly alien, what passed for speech with them might be totally different with a human.

Ralston leaned back, a cool crate along his spine, and considered how lucky they had been in speaking with the natives on Beta 7 about the chaos device. Without Westcott and his direct-connect to the computer, it would have been impossible. He had linked with their computer, then had his computer speak with the Betan one. Somewhere Ralston had seen a proof that all computer programs were, at the most elementary level, identical. Nothing could be done in one programming language that couldn't be done in another.

Certainly for computers with a binary orientation this was intuitively clear. For those based on the ternary system, it wasn't. But Ralston had asked and Westcott had told him the Betan computer was binary. On-off. True-false. Open-closed.

"Is it computer controlled?" Ralston asked aloud. "The planetoid. Is it controlled by a computer? If it is, we can get Westcott to link with it and find out all we need about the beings building it, just as we did on Beta 7."

"Might be," said Nels. "There are some interesting power-level readings. Heavy radioactivity from some of the lava spires. Unnatural, definitely chaos-induced. I think the chaos field is being generated deep inside the planetoid."

"No, Nels," said Leonore. "One probe shows strong surface forces but just inside one of the caves is nothing. If it radiated from within, the cave wouldn't give any protection. But the probe acted like a point inside a sphere with a surface charge—no charge inside. I take this to mean that inside the cavern is the chaos field source."

"Westcott," muttered Ralston. He had become so engrossed in the data collected that he had forgotten the mathematician's comatose condition. While Leonore and Nels argued over where the chaos generator was located, he rose and went back to the lounge.

Barranquilla rested quietly, her arm in a carbon composite sheath. The automedic hovered over McGhee, just as an attentive nurse might. Slim silver and plastic tubes ran to the man's arms and neck, multicolored fluids pumping in and out of his body. The bruise to the brain was serious, but Ralston felt confident that McGhee wouldn't suffer any long-term effects. The auto-doc was efficient and effective.

But for Westcott, there seemed to be no real hope. Ralston dropped beside the comatose mathematician and gently prodded him, hoping for signs of stirring. Nothing.

"Let's give you a headache," Ralston said, the idea of speaking to Westcott seeming more important than what he said. Ralston placed his hand over the infrared sensor and shut off all possible input. Westcott didn't move.

Looking over his shoulder, Ralston saw that the ship's computer was in full use. The receptor unit on the console had been turned off. Only a dull, blank gray electroceramic eye peered at him, useless without power. Three of Bernssen's team crowded close to the console and worked feverishly, discussing the toothsome tidbits of information they'd gleaned from the chaos planetoid.

Ralston moved his hand back and forth in front of Westcott's eyes. The pupils dilated slightly. Other than this, there was no response. The mathematician was trapped within his body and lacked any way of communicating with the rest of them.

"Hey," yelled Ralston as the idea struck him. "Let me use the computer. Just for a few minutes. This is important." He looked down at Westcott. "It might mean his life."

The two doing the computer analysis grumbled but relinquished the console. "For five minutes. No more, Dr. Ralston, or we have to ask Nels to get us the time."

"I'll only be a few seconds. This'll either work or it'll fail fast." Ralston turned on the computer receptor. The electroceramic eye glowed a dull red. Ralston went and positioned Westcott so that the beams matched, fixed the mathematician's head firmly with a strap, then returned to the console. There he slowly put in his request for information—directly from Westcott's brain.

"It works!" he yelped. "I've gotten through to him. Something shorted out the rest of his body's motor functions, but this works."

The others crowded close. "You're talking directly to Westcott?" asked one.

"Verd. I'm bypassing his vocal chords and going directly to his brain. We did this before in a slightly different way when we contacted the Betan."

"You are slow, so slow to understand," came Westcott's reply via the computer readout. "But I have learned so much while out of contact. I need to communicate it to you."

"Send it directly to the data bank. Code it into a block circuit so that I can pull it and examine it at length," Ralston tapped in.

"Must tell you this now. I am dying in my present state. The chaos field seized me and changed neural connections. I am permanently linked to it unless you deactivate the device. Stop it, save me."

"Deactivate it? But how? We can't even get close to it. And we don't have any missiles. This isn't a Nex warship."

"Destruction by that method isn't possible. The device must be turned off."

"How?"

"I . . . I don't know." Westcott's words wobbled across the screen, as if he were stuttering. "On the surface is the answer. You must disconnect me from it. Please, I beg you!"

"We need all the information you've gathered. Anything, Westcott. Give us all the data and your conclusions. Can you maintain contact with the computer?"

"Difficult now. So painful, but the pain is reassuring. It tells me I still have a body. I am so cut off. The chaos device has done it. My brain is alone, so alone . . ."

"The trajectory," Ralston typed into the computer. "Feed us all your work on the chaos device's trajectory. We need to know how to predict where it'll be if we're going to land on the planetoid."

"What are you saying, Ralston?" demanded a researcher who had been watching over his shoulder. "To land on the planetoid is suicide. No question about that. You'd die in minutes. Didn't the chaos field destroy the Alphans?"

"It did," said Ralston in a low voice. "But we may not have any other choice, if we want to save Westcott's life."

"Is he so bad off?" asked another. "Look at him. He's not much different than he usually is. What's he need a body for? He's pure intellect. He's certainly not human the way he direct-links with the computer."

"What would you say if it were you that needed rescuing?" Ralston shot back.

"Leave me. For the good of the team, leave me. No one person's worth risking everyone for."

"Westcott knows so much about the chaos device and perhaps even the beings who built it."

"We can find all that out—if we survive," said Barranquilla. The woman had struggled to her feet and had joined the group. Her sentiments were echoed by the ten others who had formed a tight ring around the computer console.

Ralston wasn't sure she was right. Westcott's unique skills at mathematics were necessary for full understanding of all they'd found. They might never truly know the purpose or how the chaos field functioned without Westcott.

"Is he worth risking your life for?" asked another.

To this, Ralston didn't have a good answer.

"We're not going to allow you to swoop down on the planetoid again," said Barranquilla. "We sustained enough damage the first time. And I'm not just talking about my arm. Ask the pilot. A full quarter of all ship circuits are intermittent. Try to star back to Novo Terra in this condition and we're dead."

"I know," said Ralston. "But Westcott is important."

Someone made a comment about the unimportance of a blob of protoplasm more machine than human.

Ralston wondered at his own motives for wanting to save Westcott from this living hell. Ralston could hardly stand the idea of Westcott being alive in the brain but a slave to the chaos device, with no body control, no way of communicating except through the computer—and this only sporadically. He had never even liked the mathematician. Admired his talent, yes. Loathed him, yes. Feared him, yes, that, also. Why should he risk his life to save Westcott's?

The archaeologist had no real answer for that. His emotions answered rather than his intellect. Westcott had to be saved. Even if the man didn't hold so much valuable information about the chaos device stored within his head, Ralston knew he'd try to save him. The two of them were cut off in different ways from society.

Westcott had chosen his path. For Ralston, it had come about through no fault of his own. His teaching position at the University was gone. He might be listed as being on sabbatical, but Salazar was still chancellor and would try everything possible to remove Ralston permanently from Ilium's faculty. His papers were rejected, not for content but because of Salazar's enmity.

And the Nex. Ralston couldn't forget how Slenth and Chosinth had come to him. He had promised the Nex first look at any results he obtained—that anyone on the expedition obtained. Such could only mean increased conflict between the Nex and the P'torra.

Ralston had fought on the side of the Nex. Now he viewed them as much an adversary as he did the P'torra or Chancellor Salazar.

He and Westcott shared aloneness. They drifted through space wrapped up in their own concerns. The only difference lay in the demands placed upon them. Westcott had none. Ralston carried the burden of the promise to the Nex.

Dying in the name of rescuing Westcott from imprisonment looked like a more noble way of suicide than any other Ralston might devise.

"No!" he shouted. The others stepped back, staring at him. "I won't let him die. And I won't die, either. By damn, I won't. It's not right to die like this. Too many others' lives have been taken by the chaos field. It's time to stop it right now!"

He shoved himself away from the computer and rushed to the cargo hold where Nels and Leonore worked at an almost frantic pace to get their data in some semblance of order.

"Westcott's locked in to the chaos device," he said. "The only way he knows to get free is for someone to go to the planetoid's surface, find the controls, and turn off the device."

"That's not possible," said Bernssen. "There's every reason to believe that this is a weapon of war. Why build such a weapon if the enemy could land and turn it off whenever they pleased? They'd redirect and send it back at you."

"Westcott claims that the controls exist. We're dealing with alien thought processes," said Ralston. "And we don't know that it was a weapon."

"I think we have evidence now, Michael," said Leonore. "The markings. I've had the computer working on them. Perhaps they tied in with something Westcott had left in the data banks. I don't know, but the probability that this is a weapon is 0.9 with a confidence level of ninety-five percent. It might be other things, even a paper weight for some immense and ancient desktop, but it looks good to state that it is a weapon of war."

Sweat beaded Ralston's forehead. "Have they protected the surface with armament?"

"Do they even have to?" asked Nels Bernssen. "The chaos field itself disrupts most attempts to reach it. Only two of fifteen probes reached the surface. That tells a great deal, doesn't it?"

Ralston's mind raced, then rolled over and over covering the same arguments repeatedly. Why save the mathematician? Did he dare risk his own life when he knew he'd been touched by the residual field on both Alpha 3 and Beta 5?

Intellect told him to stay safely aboard the research ship and content himself with data reduction and trying to build a picture of the race that constructed the chaos device.

Emotion told him to take a shuttle and land on the planetoid's surface, find the controls, learn to operate them, and turn it off.

"I've got to do it," Ralston said. "I'll take the shuttle. Cram in all the spare equipment you can find, Leonore. I'll relay everything possible back as I descend to the surface. Once there, I doubt if much will continue working."

"You may not last longer than a few minutes," said Bernssen. "Remember your seizure? Being this near the source of the chaos may kill you outright. This *is* a weapon."

"I know. I'll land near the caverns where the markings are. They must be a 'Keep Out' sign. That's exactly the spot I want. With luck, I can be in, look around, and see what needs to be done before I keel over."

"Flop over like a fish out of water, you mean," Leonore said sourly. "I don't want you going, Michael. As head of the expedition, I can order you to stay."

"You can," Ralston said. "But you won't. I know what I'm doing. And I'm going down."

The words had barely come from Michael Ralston's mouth when he realized that he had just committed himself to a course that could end only in death—his own death.

SIXTEEN

"BOTH SUPERVISORS?" ASKED Michael Ralston, eyebrows rising in surprise. "Shouldn't you keep one, just to be sure that you can monitor the working probes?"

Leonore laughed. "Michael, Michael, we want to get back in one piece. Equipment doesn't matter. People do."

For a moment, Ralston started to thank her for the kind thought, then understood what she'd said.

"*We* want to get back? What's this 'we' you're talking about? I'm going alone."

"Sorry, Michael, that's too dangerous." Leonore Disa glowed with excitement. "As head of this part of the expedition, you don't think I'd let you go alone and have all the fun, do you?"

"There's not going to be any fun," he said, grimness in his voice. "I'll probably not make it back alive. One suicide per expedition is enough. Keep one supervisor and monitor me closely. That might tell more than a random walk route for a probe across the planetoid's surface."

"Here," said Nels Bernssen, heaving the second supervisor into the shuttle. He pushed Ralston aside and began installing it. When he finished, he flopped into a tiny acceleration couch that barely held his bulky body. "You going to pilot or am I?"

"You, too? No, absolutely not," Ralston said forcefully. "You're not going, too."

"As the one responsible for how the funds are spent, I'm

in charge of the expedition. Leonore's in charge of her part of it. You're the hired help. Want us to leave you behind?''

"Leonore, Nels, please!"

"Stop whining or we *will* leave you behind. We've got to launch in less than ten minutes if we want an optimum time trajectory to the planetoid's surface. The pilot's worked out the round trip for us and I've got it on four block circuits." Leonore patted a small bag hanging at her waist. "Each of us will take one. The fourth will go into the steering computer. If anything chaotic happens to it, each of us has a chance of getting back with their spare."

Ralston's head spun. Everything moved too quickly around him. He had intended this to be a solo mission, quick in and even quicker to find the chaos weapon's controls. Nothing else mattered, if he wanted to free Westcott from his domination by the field.

"Maybe we should call it off. One of the others said that no single life is worth risking everyone's for."

"Locked inside Westcott's head is a phenomenal amount of data," said Bernssen. "We need it. No one else can duplicate what he's learned about the strange attractor, the chaos field, the history of it, the people who built it. He's unique in that." Nels had hit Ralston's weakness: the race that constructed the chaos device.

"Three of us needn't go."

"I'm going because Leonore is. Since I'm the primary investigator for the expedition and supposed to make decisions, no one overturns me in these matters."

"And I'm going because you are, Michael," said Leonore. She smiled wickedly. "Even if you backed out, I might still go. This is an opportunity no one else has ever had and I'm not going to miss it." She clasped his upper arms and squeezed hard. "Knowledge isn't always advanced safely. We know the risks and have prepared for them the best we can. We might lose our lives."

"Chances are damned good we will," said Ralston.

"But there's a chance also that we won't, that we'll learn even more about the chaos field and its generation and its builders. We all know this opportunity might not happen again."

"You're right. We still haven't disproved Westcott's notion that the field will self-destruct due to its own nature. Who knows what would happen to him if that happened. We've got to take this chance, no matter how slim it seems," Ralston said, resigned to having the others along. Out loud, he tried to dissuade them, but deep down he was happy for their courage and company. He might need that more than any technical expertise on their parts.

Ralston reached over and hit the call button to connect him with Gonzales. "We're going airtight now. Launch window still open?" he asked the pilot.

"That crazy set of coordinates Westcott put into the computer is proving damned accurate," came the pilot's voice. "The planetoid is surging and decelerating till the saints won't have it. I can maintain a parallel course for another ten hours, if Westcott's numbers stay accurate."

"We'll be back before then," said Ralston. He silently added, *Or we won't be back at all.*

Ralston settled into the couch. The tingling in his arms had stopped for the moment. The lightheadedness he experienced might be due to nerves and not the effect of the chaos field. He didn't know, but it would bear watching.

"All set?" he called out to Leonore and Nels.

"We're strapped in. Kick us free whenever you want," said Bernssen.

"Good-bye it is, then!" Ralston rammed home the throttle and sent the shuttle leaping from its bay in the side of the starship. The acceleration crushed him down like a giant invisible fist until he turned over the course control to the precomputed trajectory locked within the block circuit.

Lateral blasts threw him to one side, then the shuttle corrected its course and they settled into a more sedate trip.

"We'll be down in less than an hour," Ralston said. "The ship's flying a braid pattern orbit around the planetoid, dipping in, then surging out."

"Ten hours?" asked Leonore. "We're down in one, have eight, and then one back. Not much time to look around."

"One down, five to look," corrected Ralston. "And maybe faster, if I can get to the controls and shut down the field."

"But . . ."

"But nothing," cut in Ralston. "We're already dying. We may not feel it, but we are. What took centuries to affect the

Alphans will be happening to us in minutes. We're not passing near the field, we'll be as close to it as possible—in it."

"I'm still getting reports back from the two probes, Michael," said Leonore, not arguing with him over the time for exploration. "Every tiny glitch is being recorded and backed up. So far, neither supervisor is showing any trouble. I'm running the internal self-check every five minutes."

"Good. Nels? Your equipment still functioning?"

"Verd. Fantastic readings I'm getting. The field strength indications show that it varies randomly. We're in a period of low intensity now."

"Let's hope we stay there," said Ralston.

He worried for the duration of their flight, fidgeting and nervously tapping his fingers across the controls. He wanted to stand and pace, but the shuttle had been laden so heavily with equipment that little room had been left for such a show of nerves.

"Here it comes," Ralston finally called. "Got visual on the front viewscreen."

"Also got malfunction on the steering," chimed in Leonore. "Need any help?"

"Take over for me," ordered Ralston. Leonore was a better pilot than he was—and his arms had begun twitching hard enough to make it difficult to pilot. Ralston slipped his hands under a restraining strap and tried unsuccessfully to control his spastic movements.

"Here we go, then," said Leonore. Deft, small, strong hands worked on the controls, fine-tuning, adjusting, giving instructions to the computer to land them less than a hundred meters from a tiny cluster of lava upjuts covered with the markings a probe had photographed and relayed back before going dead.

"There. Touchdown," she said.

"You pilot better than Ralston," said Nels in admiration. "Hell, you pilot better than I do."

"One advantage to growing up rich. I've always had my own ship to dart around in." Leonore swung free and began to fasten up her helmet for the preliminary exploration.

The only exploration, Ralston corrected. There would be no methodical, painstaking examination of the ground, of the lava pillars, of their immediate surroundings for artifacts or other remnants of the civilization constructing the device. As he'd been forced to do so many times before, this would be more hit-and-run archaeology. Land, photograph wildly in all directions, take what wasn't too large to carry, then leave in a hurry.

He hated it but there was nothing else he could do. Better to obtain a few bits of data than none.

"I never knew you could pilot, much less do it this well," said Bernssen.

"We can talk about it later," Leonore said. She ran her fingers around the edge of her helmet, fastening it down expertly. "How's the suit radio doing?"

"Fine," said Ralston. He glanced down at his arms. The muscle contractions had stopped. To Nels he said, "Keep me posted on the field strength."

"Still at a minimum, though we went through a small increase coming in."

Ralston had feared this. The field strength determined how much—or how little—control he had over his own body.

"What are you measuring when you say 'field strength'?"

"Magnetic field," said Bernssen.

"Can we use it to find the generator?"

"Maybe. I'm not sure exactly what we're supposed to be doing," said Bernssen.

"Nobody's sure," said Ralston. "So let's do whatever it is we're supposed to do but don't know about yet."

He got his feet under him and gingerly put his weight down. His legs held. No quivering in them. With more confidence, Ralston fastened the hood of his spacesuit and checked out the radio. Nels did likewise.

"We're all set to do some archaeology," said Leonore. "But first, here're the block circuits with our programmed course." She handed each of them a precious block of yttrium aluminum garnet ceramic. "Keep 'em safe and let's hope we don't have to use any but the one that's in the board."

"Send out the probes," Ralston ordered. "We want a quick check for radiation, poison gases, loose dust, and pits."

"All the probes are gone," said Leonore.

"Do you mean sent out or *gone*?"

"Not working. Out of commission. *Muerto*."

"I get the picture. We're on our own. Carry what you can and let's get going." Ralston checked his chronometer. "We've been down almost eight minutes."

"Field strength rising," said Bernssen.

Ralston knew. His hands shook so hard that he dropped the IR camera he'd taken from an overhead rack. The shakes passed and Ralston indicated that they should leave.

They descended to the base of the shuttle. The lava had flowed near the rocket exhausts and left tiny puddles of bubbling rock. They skirted the minor destruction their landing had caused and went directly to the lava pillars. Leonore chuckled to herself as she began photographing. She soon quieted down and started recording a long verbal description of the markings they found.

Ralston had insisted that they use technology as primitive as possible. The fewer sophisticated parts, the less likely their records were of being destroyed. He mistrusted the block circuits; one small magnetic domain realigned might destroy huge segments of information. Audio recording was old-fashioned but durable. Ralston hated having to use the block circuit camera but they hadn't brought along an old silver halide film camera and there hadn't been time to make one and the film it required.

Nels Bernssen crouched down on the surface and took readings of anything and everything with his hand-held analyzer.

While they worked, Ralston wandered. The markings were bright yellow against the dark black of the jagged lava. He didn't attempt to interpret; he allowed himself to drift. The markings appeared to indicate one particular cave opening.

Ralston went inside.

Barely had he entered when a seizure grabbed total control of his body. Ralston flopped about, knowing what happened and feeling degraded, embarrassed, outraged. Clenching his teeth tightly to keep from biting his tongue, Ralston slammed hard against the cavern wall. Arms reached out and closed on a small boulder. He rolled over and over, clinging to the rock as if his life depended on it. When the seizure passed, Ralston lay panting.

"Michael! What's wrong?" came Leonore's cry in his ears.

"I had a seizure. My mind didn't go blank but I couldn't do much more than flop around. I'm all right now."

"Nels, come on. We'll go with him."

"No!" called Ralston. Too late. Both Leonore and Nels stepped inside the cavern, but for them the experience was different. Wildly different.

"It's so pretty!" cried Nels. "I never imagined anything like this. I can smell colors. And hear taste."

Ralston stared at them. They experienced the sensory confusion he did during star shifts.

"I can hear the darkness," said Leonore. "It's singing such a mournful song. How it hurts. Oh, I want to help it, but I can't. I don't know how."

"Stay where you are, please," pleaded Ralston. "I'm not confused the way you are. Stay outside and monitor my signals." He stood and forced calm on his trembling hands. This time his shaking came from fear rather than chaos-induced epilepsy.

"You don't see this? Oh, I'm sorry for you, Michael."

Ralston shoved both Leonore and Nels from the mouth of the cavern. They fell heavily, lying on the stony ground for a few minutes, shaken and unable to move.

"I have no idea how I know it, but this is the control center," Ralston said. "What was a hindrance for me before looks like an asset now. I experienced the sensory disorientation during shifts and you didn't. This is scrambling your senses and not touching mine." He dropped to his knees, intense pain shooting through his head, turning the world red before his eyes.

"The chaos field is working on me. I feel it," he said. "We won't even have five hours. I've got to find the controls and turn them off. I've got to."

He spoke more to convince himself that he could fight than to inform the others of his intentions. Ralston stumbled forward, going deeper into the darkness of the cavern. The walls turned into liquid-smooth obsidian beneath his fingers; he ran one hand along to hold himself upright. A hundred meters into the cave, Ralston remembered the IR camera dangling around his neck.

Lifting it to his eye, he peered through the sights. The darkness vanished, replaced by the eerie infrared world of heat. Brilliant plumes rose from the floor of a chamber he hadn't even realized existed. Not five paces away Ralston saw a steep precipice, dropping two meters to a rocky pit. In the center of the circular pit stood a solid column.

"The colors," he muttered. "The colors! Around the column of lava are all the colors of the rainbow—more! I've never seen such beauty. It can't be natural. It's too . . . too fantastic!"

"Michael, are you experiencing the scrambling we did? That you do during a shift?"

"No," he said. "I can see heat rising around the spire through the camera. But the colors are there. They shift and dance and change. They're like electronic veils of aurora, some type of coronal discharge."

"I'm not picking up any electrical disturbances," came Bernssen's voice, much weaker now than Ralston would have thought. He'd traveled less than two hundred meters from the cave mouth to this point. "Are you all right?"

"Fine, fine," said Ralston, distracted. He slid down the slope, taking care not to tear his spacesuit on the sharp lava rock edges. Staring up at the gauzy veils glittering around him, he walked to the central spire and laid his hand on it.

Warmth flowed through the glove and into his hand—and a convulsion struck him so hard that it sent him tumbling head over heels. Ralston moaned as the sharp rocks jabbed into his side. He carefully rolled to hands and knees, trying not to puncture his suit. The fabric was impervious to any but the most insistent attempts to breach it, but Ralston wanted to take as few chances as possible.

One epileptic seizure could unlock the ferocious power in his muscles and cast him hard enough against a rock to puncture the suit.

He looked up and saw the rainbows of delicate colors fluttering about his head, as if caught on gentle summer breezes. In the airlessness of the chaos-wracked planetoid, that wasn't possible. Ralston stood and returned to the spire.

"I've found the controls," he said with certainty. "I have no idea how they reached them, unless they flew. The spire holding the controls might be climbed, if I'm lucky."

Intense sizzling static reached his ears. Through it, he made out Nels' voice. ". . . Leonore's had a seizure . . ." were the only words he caught.

"Get back to the ship. I'll follow when I can," he ordered. But Ralston had no confidence that his words weren't similarly garbled by the rise in static. If that meant the electrical field changed abruptly, the magnetic field—the only indicator they had—might be changing, too. And that meant a new bout of chaotic troubles.

Ralston brushed his fingers across the rocky spire. No sensation. The archaeologist took a deep breath, found hand-and footholds, and began his way up.

"I hope these *are* the controls," he said, more to himself than to Bernssen. He had blundered into this spot simply because of the yellow markings on the rock. This might be anything—it might be an exhaust or a projector for a death beam or any of a thousand other things.

But something deep within Ralston told him these were the controls for the chaos field.

Scampering as fast as he could, he got to the top of the spire. His heart sank. He had expected to find a box with neat rows of switches and readouts. He found nothing but the rocky tip of the lava pillar.

All around him floated veils of color, changing from red to blue to yellow and through every possible hue between.

"The colors," he said reverently. "The real colors of chaos."

Ralston clutched at himself when the colors flowed into a crimson curtain. His arms flopped as if he tried to take to wing and fly. As the color changed slowly to a more sedate olive green, control of his limbs returned.

"They must act as an indicator of what's happening," he said. Ralston took pictures, changing the spectral sensitivity of the block camera. He had no idea if he recorded anything at all. He could only try.

"The colors of chaos," he mused. He remembered—so long ago!—back on Novo Terra in Westcott's lab how the mathematician had plotted the chaos equations visually. The blacks were stable points, the strange attractors. The brightest reds were the most unstable points, the ones going to infinity in the complex plane the most rapidly.

Ralston looked around and saw the dazzling display as an immense imaginary number graph. He had no idea of the equation being plotted, but it resembled the one Westcott had generated. Nodes and peaks formed, sharp singularities and entire stable areas stretched out.

"All the chaos equations are being generated," he said softly, almost as if the builders might hear and appreciate his understanding, "and this shows what damage is being caused!"

The colors swirled in sharp, saw-toothed patterns, then worked through every conceivable shade and shape.

"That's exactly like the one Westcott plotted," Ralston said, noting a particular pattern forming. "The one for the radioactive decay." Ralston felt stirrings deep within his skull. He held at bay the panic and tried to guess how the colors would progress.

They followed the exact pattern he'd predicted!

Through the static came Bernssen's voice, much clearer now. "Heavy radiation. The surface is turning hot, Michael. We've got to get away."

Ralston began thinking of the colors as deepening, turning darker—more stable.

"Is the radiation level decreasing?" he asked.

"Yes, but how'd you know that?"

"I've got the controls. I don't know what to do with them exactly, but I am at the controls."

"Turn off the field. Don't worry about learning the controls," cried Bernssen, "just turn it off! I've got to get Leonore back to the ship. She hasn't come out of the seizure."

"We're more susceptible than you are. We were touched by the residual effects on Beta 5 and on Alpha 3 through the telepathic projectors," said Ralston, more interested in how to shift the colors and their patterns than in Bernssen's problems.

"Turn it off!" pleaded Nels Bernssen.

Ralston saw a new shape forming in the space around him. Marching black "S" shapes moved to a jerky beat. The colorful iteration repeated as far as Ralston could see.

"Got contact from the ship," came Bernssen's voice over the spacesuit speakers. "The sun's preparing to go nova. It's been here long enough to cause the sun to explode. We've got to leave *now*, Michael."

"It's the pattern," Ralston said. "This pattern induces novas. The other conformal mapping causes or suppresses radioactivity. Which one causes the epilepsy?"

He played with the colors, changing them by his thoughts to a brown and finally finding true blackness. Ralston wondered if the Bernssen Condition for novas had vanished. He thought it had gone with the colorful pattern.

New and disturbing patterns appeared, almost flashing past him before he could see them. Ralston closed his eyes and concentrated on the color black. Only in blackness was there stability. The attractors were black; those were stable points.

If all turned black and stable, that meant the chaos device was inactivated. It had to.

Ticklings at the fringes of his mind told Ralston that he skirted at the edge of real control. Much of the spacial plotting of the chaos equations turned black, but enough didn't to let Ralston know some randomness still occurred.

"There, there, more black, less pattern and more stability," he almost chanted. "Darkness, darkness, be my guide. Stability!"

The patterns moderated, turned quiescent and dark. Whatever generated the field calmed and began to sleep.

Then came the random shift to an exploding fountain of colors, bright yellows and greens and blues and oranges and reds, that Ralston couldn't control.

The froth of color shot upward, heading for infinity. And along with it, Ralston felt control slipping from his body. This was the pattern he'd dreaded most.

This was the pattern of personal destruction. Ralston lost consciousness and flopped off the rocky spire, muscles locked in the rictus of epileptic seizure.

SEVENTEEN

"So COLD, TOO cold," mumbled Michael Ralston. He felt as if he floated, drifting disembodied in a sea of ice. He kicked feebly, his legs finding only the rough-edged shards of lava. "Arms. Can't move my arms." He struggled until strong hands shook him.

"Stop that. I'm trying to get you out of here. We've got to return to the shuttle right away."

Ralston thought that his senses had been scrambled by the chaos field. He reached out with his mind, as he'd done before, to adjust the flow, to change the mathematical progression of the colors, to alter their confusing multitudes of infinities. Only glaring white light struck his eyes. He squinted and one hand rose to shield his eyes.

"Nels?"

"Stand up. I can't drag you any farther. I thought I could, but this has taken too much out of me."

Ralston's eyes adjusted to Bernssen's brilliant headlamp beams. He sat up and reached for his face, only to find the spacesuit helmet in the way. Memories returned in disconnected trickles, a little here, more there. But it confused him so.

"We're still in the cavern?"

"About fifty meters out. I got Leonore back to the shuttle when she had the seizure, strapped her down and sedated her, then went after you. By the time I'd reached the cave entrance the field had died down and I didn't get the sensory confusion.''

"I turned it off," Ralston said in a low voice. Louder, "I turned it off. *I shut down the chaos field!*"

"Verd, of course you did," said Nels. No hint of belief carried in his words.

"But I did! I stood on that spire. You saw the lava spire? I got to the top of it and saw the colors dancing around me like veils and sprites and exotic figures. Somehow, I managed to attune myself with it, and I *controlled* it."

"It's not going to come back on unexpectedly?"

"I don't know. I don't think it will, but if it does, I can turn it off again."

"Fine, fine, but we've got to get to the shuttle. The launch window is closing rapidly on us. We've got to blast off within twenty minutes or we won't have enough fuel to return to the ship."

"But there's plenty of time. We had ten hours . . ." Ralston glanced at his chronometer. "This can't be right. The chaos field changed it, speeded it up."

"It's right," confirmed Bernssen. "You were inside the cavern for almost the full ten hours. Leonore and I waited outside for almost six before she had the seizure."

"Time flowed differently for me. I spent only a few minutes on the spire." Ralston heaved himself to his feet, wobbled, and then took a few tentative steps. When he didn't fall over, he began walking slowly, each step a major accomplishment.

By the time they exited the cave, Ralston had regained much of his strength. He stopped and looked around the barren planetoid. So many secrets were locked away under this rocky surface. He had turned off the field but he hadn't seen the mechanism creating it. Westcott had claimed it was a concept rather than an actual device. Ralston didn't know—and couldn't speak authoritatively even though he'd experienced the field's effects at their source.

There hadn't been time to explore, to photograph, to learn. Never enough time!

"I know, Michael," said Nels. "What we did in the six

hours you were inside wasn't complete. Leonore complained bitterly about how inadequate our exploration was.''

"Did any of the probes come back to life when I turned off the chaos field?"

Bernssen shrugged. "I wasn't interested in that. Only in seeing that Leonore was resting comfortably."

They reached the shuttle. At the top of the ladder, Ralston stopped and looked back over his shoulder. A tear formed in the corners of his eyes. What secrets the race that built this planetoid-sized weapon had. And they could have been his!

He tumbled into the airlock and then helped Nels struggle inside. They impatiently waited for air to pump in. Their helmets zipped off and stored, the two men hurried to the cramped cockpit. Leonore lay on the rear couch, snoring softly. Almost hesitantly, Ralston took her pulse: steady and slow.

''She seems all right. We'll have to hook her up to the automedic to be certain.''

"I had nightmares of brain aneurisms and strokes from the exposure to the chaos field," said Nels. He stood beside her, shifting back and forth uncertainly.

Ralston dropped into his couch and reached over to check the supervisor. Dead, a victim of chaos. Its electronic circuits had suffered the equivalent fate that Leonore's biologic system had. He turned and looked at the second supervisor. It had fared better and still functioned. A self-check of its circuits showed most to be operational—and four probes had reactivated after the chaos field had been turned off. Ralston hit the control toggle that stored the information in the supervisor's block circuits, then made spare copies.

"Let's get out of here," he said. His fingers seemed numb on the controls, but he fought to keep his concentration on the work and not his personal condition.

"What's wrong, Michael?"

"It's the block circuit with our programmed escape course. It's dead." Ralston reached up to the shuttle's control panel and popped out the destroyed block and tossed it aside. He pulled out the one Leonore had given him and inserted it.

It was dead, too.

"Here's mine," said Bernssen, handing over the tiny ceramic computer block.

The engines vented throaty roars and lights began flashing, but it took only seconds for Ralston to see that Bernssen's block circuit had also been a fatality to the chaos-induced randomness.

"We can wing it," said Nels. "You fly, I'll compute."

"We're too close to the edge of the window," said Ralston. He held back the panic rising within. He had turned off the most fearsome weapon the galaxy had ever seen and now a broken block circuit might kill him. He refused to die because of it. He wouldn't die!

"Fuel level is critical," said Nels, looking at the readout. "But if we can get near enough to the ship, they can maneuver and pick us up."

"Oxygen is critical, too. Look at the indicators."

"That's impossible. We have full tanks. Enough for weeks."

"Sniff." Ralston opened a valve and jerked away when the gas spewed forth.

"Smells like garlic."

"The chaos field turned the oxygen into ozone. Must have done the same to the fuel blocks. We'll be running short on both oxygen and fuel if we don't make rendezvous the first time."

"Can you do it?"

"No." Ralston knew his limits as a pilot. Leonore might be able to, but he couldn't, not now that their block circuits had fallen prey to chaos. Ralston leaned back when he thought of the woman, then laughed. "What idiots we are. There's one more chance. Leonore's block. Get it."

Nels fumbled in his haste to pull the block circuit from the sleeping woman's carrying pouch. With a comic reverence, he carried it in cupped hands to Ralston.

It slid into the control panel. Lights again blossomed. And the navigation computer chuckled merrily to itself, finding acceptable data to guide the ship.

Ralston almost fainted with relief. He sat up and began to prepare for the launch. "All set," he called to Nels. "Make sure you're both fastened down tight. This is going to be a rough trip. We're just past the last computed launch window."

"Can you contact the ship and let them know we're coming?"

The red light on the control panel told Ralston that most of their communications circuitry had died in the chaos field.

"We'll be all right," he assured the physicist. Ralston kept repeating the same words over and over to convince himself. It didn't help.

The kick from the rockets drove him back into the couch. Ralston fought to keep from passing out. Although the acceleration wasn't that intense, his battered body wanted to quit. Only force of will kept him going. Ralston watched the readouts through half-hooded eyes. The block circuit had them on the proper course.

He hoped it was the right course. He couldn't know the details, but it seemed right. Only when Ralston thought they were safely en route did he relax and let the waves of blackness wash over him. He passed out.

"How long has it been?" he asked. Ralston forced his eyes to open and focus on Nels Bernssen. The physicist huddled over the control panel and ran his fingers almost lovingly over the switches that determined their fate.

"Too long. We boosted for almost an hour and then ran out of fuel."

Ralston felt an icy spike driving hard into his guts. They'd left the research ship with enough fuel for a dozen trips to the planetoid and back.

"The effects of the chaos," Nels confirmed. "Something happened to the chemical makeup of the fuel blocks. Some fired, most didn't. Engines shut down to keep from uneven burns."

"The same as what happened to our oxygen." Ralston's nose wrinkled at the harsh ozone odor lingering from the brief venting while they were still on the planetoid's surface.

"It must be. We're drifting without rockets, and we have less than an hour's worth of oxygen."

"And we can't contact the ship," Ralston finished the litany of despair. "Most of the equipment on the shuttle's not working and we're drifting now." He leaned back, eyes closed. It seemed anticlimactic for his life to end in this way.

Of all the archaeologists working in the field, he had made the most astounding discoveries, had discovered lost worlds and cultures, watched them snuffed out in a blast of chaos-fueled nova, and had capped his career with finding the source of the most devastating weapon in the universe.

"There is a bright side to all this," said Nels.

"You might as well tell me. I can use it."

"We don't have to write any papers or reveal what we've discovered about the chaos weapon to the Nex."

"Bright spot," muttered Ralston. Maybe this *was* the best they could hope for. Keeping the awesome power of the chaos field from Nex, P'torra, and human war fleets might rank as his major accomplishment.

Only no one would ever know. Ralston glanced around the shuttle cockpit that would be his eternal tomb. He'd hoped for more.

"How's Leonore?"

"Still in a coma," said Nels, worry in his voice. "But she's resting comfortably and doesn't seem to be in pain."

"She'll come out of this all right. We all will," Ralston said.

Even as he spoke, the air clogged his nose and throat with its staleness. He coughed and rubbed his watering eyes. Every muscle in his body ached horribly.

"Want something to eat?" asked Nels. "We have enough, unless it's been chaotically changed into poison."

"Might be a boon, if it has," said Ralston. "The air's getting close, isn't it?" He coughed again.

"While you were out, I checked all the tanks. The main tank's more ozone than oxygen. The secondary tanks are exhausted. What's in the shuttle now is all we have."

"Spacesuits?"

"Another few hours each, but without maneuvering rockets, what's the difference?"

Ralston closed his eyes, temples pounding hard and his heart feeling as if it would leap from his chest.

"Fire," he said. "A torch. Can you put together a plasma torch?"

"We have a couple welding lasers aboard." For a few seconds Nels Bernssen didn't understand, then a big grin spread across his face. "I'll get it. Want to open the oxygen valve?"

"How dangerous is this going to be?"

"What's the difference?" asked the physicist. He returned with a welding laser, adjusted the twin beams to intersect at the precise point where the ozone would exhaust from its tank.

Ralston opened the valve slowly and let a small stream out. The laser superheated the ozone and broke it down into oxygen. What other combustion products were formed would be removed by the shuttle's efficient filtering system.

"Enough for the moment," Nels said. "We've got enough to last a day or two before it gets stuffy again."

"The mechanical filter's not likely to quit on us," said Ralston. The air tasted metallic on his tongue, but it carried none of the choking ozone vapor.

"We've got food, air, and all the time in the world. What should we do with it?" asked Nels. The man's tone was light, but Ralston noticed that he kept glancing toward Leonore, worried for her.

"Data reduction? We've got enough to work on for a lifetime." Ralston instantly regretted his choice of words.

"I think I'll take some more data," said Nels. "I never did like the dogwork of actually sifting through all the numbers to find the one or two gems."

The physicist settled in front of a spectrometer and aimed its optics at the solar system's primary. Ralston lay back on the couch, eyes closed, mind racing. They couldn't contact the research ship because they had no idea where it was—and with their rockets useless, reaching the ship would be impossible. How could they skirt all those impossibles and survive? He worked over one scheme after another, each more implausible than the one before.

"Michael, I've just finished with the first pictures of the star."

"And?" asked Ralston.

"The Bernssen condition is present. This sun's going nova soon. I'd say within a few months."

Ralston accepted the news calmly. They'd be dead long

before the cleansing plumes of superheated plasma licked outward in the star's death throes.

"That means the chaos weapon will be destroyed. There's no way it can orbit free of the system in time, not at sublight speeds."

"I never had the impression that it traveled faster than light," said Ralston. "It might have, but there's so much we will never know about it." He lay back, quiet now, reflecting on fate. The chaos weapon might be decaying, as Westcott had calculated, but it didn't matter. It had sent such a jolt of chaos into this star's stellar furnace that it couldn't escape the system before being destroyed.

It would die in fires of its own creation. A fitting end, thought Ralston.

"There's not any chance to make a primitive radio and contact the ship," said Nels.

"What?" Ralston's chain of thought had been broken by this unexpected comment.

"I'd considered bollixing together a radio and trying to set up an interference field that the ship might find, but with the sun's instability at such a level, it'd drown out any noise we might make."

"It might not have been powerful enough, in any case. There's not much laying around loose in the way of equipment." Almost all equipment aboard the shuttle came in prepackaged modular form. Tearing it apart would avail them only broken equipment, not valuable parts to be reconstructed into life-saving gadgets.

"Most of it isn't working right, anyway," said Nels. The man slumped back in a couch, tiredness permanently etched on his face. "But we can't give up, can we?"

"I can't," said Ralston. "I'll keep thinking about it until something occurs to me. I don't believe the pilot would abandon us."

"They might decide to leave if they've noticed the increasing instability in the stellar furnace," Nels said.

"We're supposed to find ways out, not invent new problems. But that's an easy one to get around. Would you leave a newly formed nova unless you had to immediately? No, you'd stay as long as you could to study it. So will McGhee and Barranquilla and the others.''

"Barranquilla's in charge since I'm gone," he said. "She wouldn't want to leave until the first hard gamma and x-rays struck the hull of the ship. Nothing's more important to her than her magnetic moment measurements.''

They talked idly, occasionally drifting up to check the few readouts still functioning.

Time ceased to have meaning, although Ralston frequently checked his chronometer. Sometimes only a few minutes had passed. Other times showed long hours. Both intervals seemed identical to him. And always he worried over how to contact the research ship. He'd insisted that Bernssen set up monitoring equipment to automatically alert them if the ship neared, but even Ralston had to admit the chances of this happening accidentally were close to zero.

The shuttle had started for a rendezvous point with the research ship, but when the engines had quit, their course was directly out of the system. No planets orbited nearby, they detected no asteroids or small bits of matter, and the chaos planetoid hurled itself away, far away from any chance of returning.

Four days of drifting. Five. Eight. Ralston and Bernssen spent most of their time asleep. Leonore's condition did not improve, but it did not worsen. Of the three Ralston envied her the most. She knew nothing of their peril—or the initial boredom followed by increasing realization that they would die.

Ralston awakened, nose clogged and the shuttle cockpit wavering behind his watery eyes. He'd managed to get a cold. Without the auto-doc he had no real chance of getting over it before they all died.

Ralston laughed hard at this, then laughed to the point of hysteria. He had reconciled himself to dying, or lied to himself well enough that he believed he had. But to die with a head cold? That was an indignity he wouldn't tolerate.

Nels had tried to put together any number of communication devices. None worked. Ralston knew he had no chance of succeeding where the physicist had failed, but checking the instruments now and then made him feel he was doing something useful.

"I'm not going to die with a cold. I'm not!"

He wiped his eyes and stared into the eyepiece of Bernssen's spectrometer. It showed a band pattern unlike any he'd ever seen before. Nels had been watching the star and Ralston had accustomed himself to the light and dark bands. This was different, more intense.

"Nels?" he called. "What do you make of this? Is the sun going to explode?"

The physicist heaved himself up from the couch beside Leonore and stared at the spectral pattern. His mouth opened, then snapped shut hard.

"What is it?"

"That's the spectrum for a rocket exhaust."

"The research ship? But how?"

"I don't know. I just don't know. Even if they were hunting for us, they'd have no way of finding where we'd gone."

But they had been found. An hour later, magnetic docking lines from the research ship slammed into the airlock and slowly pulled the shuttle into its docking bay.

EIGHTEEN

"WESTCOTT!" CRIED MICHAEL RALSTON, seeing the mathematician waiting for them inside the research ship's airlock. "You're all right! You came out of the coma!"

"Verd, I am well again." Westcott looked curiously uneasy. His watery eyes refused to meet Ralston's. "I want to thank you. You saved my life."

"What? Oh, turning off the chaos field? That did it?"

"It did. Once the power of the chaos faded, I was able to fight against the residual bonds holding me. It took almost a week, but after that, I returned to normal."

Ralston refused to comment about what was normal for the computer-linked mathematician. Instead, he said, "You're the one who started looking for us, aren't you? It looks as if we all owe *you* a debt of thanks."

Westcott watched emotionlessly as Leonore Disa was carried from the shuttle, Nels Bernssen following closely. "It posed a problem requiring considerable thought and computation. No one else is capable of solving such a complex set of equations."

"How did you know where to look for us? Or even that we wouldn't be able to contact you? You could have assumed we were dead on the planetoid."

"Barranquilla and the others noted the Bernssen Condition and the incipient nova. I, naturally, knew that the chaos field had collapsed because of the skewed time between chaos introduction and the ultimate effect. The onslaught of this

197

nova had to mean success on your part. The collapse of the chaos field would result in a sudden burst, then nothing. Because of this burst, the nova was initiated and I knew that your equipment would, in the main, have failed. That would include the most chaotically 'fragile,' all the communication and computer equipment.

"Further reflection told of potential problems with your solid fuel blocks. Chemical reactions would not proceed properly near the center of the chaos field."

"But how did you find us?"

Westcott smiled. Ralston wasn't sure he liked the cadaverous expression.

"The chaos equations. I simply added in equipment failure to possible courses and random direction of takeoff from the planetoid to get the most volumes of space."

"And you sailed straight to us, just like that." Ralston marveled at what he had to rate as luck, in spite of knowing the mathematics—and Westcott's genius—behind their rescue.

"Not exactly. We searched seven different volumes of space before finding you."

Ralston laughed, then stepped forward to shake Westcott's hand. He reached out and collapsed, the strain finally taking its toll on him.

"Leonore is up and around?" he asked Nels Bernssen. The tall blond's head bobbed up and down, his smile almost dazzling.

"The auto-doc had her fixed up in less than a day. She'd suffered a series of strokes on the planetoid, nothing too dangerous. She still lisps a little, but that will go away after a bit more therapy. But how are you feeling? You look a world better."

"Feel it," said Ralston. He stretched and sat up in the bunk. He knew he had to be on the mend. Already, his cabin seemed constricting to him, too small, too plain. "In spite of being in the center of the chaos field, not much happened to me physically. The automedic has been whirring away. What problems remain are the ones I've always had."

Ralston saw Bernssen's worried expression and asked, "What's wrong?"

"Nothing, actually. It's just that you were unconscious for so long."

"Long? But it's only been a few hours."

"It's been close to two weeks. We've held off starring back to Novo Terra because of your condition."

"Starring back? Why?"

"The sun. You remember it was going nova? Westcott's calculated that we have less than four days left before it explodes." Bernssen held up his hand to forestall Ralston's objection. "He was wrong before, but then he didn't have the data from the planetoid. He's been refining his solution sets. This time we have physical evidence that he's right. And he measured the chaotic burst that set off the Bernssen Condition."

"Why worry about me?"

"We didn't want to shift and have your senses scrambled. The auto-doc thought it might kill you, in light of what happened on the planetoid."

Ralston snorted in disgust. He felt great. Nothing could harm him now. He'd fought chaos and won!

"Have you been studying the planetoid?" Ralston asked.

"It's been difficult. Its course took it almost directly across the disk of the star. Solar activity blotted out most of our sensitive measurements."

"Then it'll be destroyed in the nova?"

"It would have been destroyed within a week, anyway. We were lucky to reach it when we did. Westcott is sure that it was already decaying, fading to nothing all by itself."

Ralston sank back on his bunk, a curious mixture of feelings fighting for supremacy within. The opportunity to study it for archaeological evidence had passed. For that, he mourned. But the chaos weapon would never again threaten entire solar systems and bring about the woe that it had for untold millennia.

But the knowledge that was being destroyed in the blink of an eye!

Ralston reconsidered this lost knowledge. What they hadn't learned, they couldn't pass along to the Nex. And if the Nex didn't have it, then neither did the P'torra. That didn't reduce the chance for war, but it removed a weapon from both sides' arsenals that neither could control, much less understand.

"How much has Westcott learned?"

"That's hard to say," said Bernssen. "A great deal. We've all got mountains of data to sift through, and it will be career making for us all. Epoch making for science, too. Every field of endeavor will be affected. Biology, physics, mathematics." Bernssen smiled. "Archaeology. Leonore's been working on a computer simulation of the planetoid and has learned a great deal about the race that constructed the chaos weapon."

Ralston's heart pounded with excitement and a flush rose to his cheeks.

"I've got to see what she's done."

Bernssen pushed him gently back into the bunk. "Later. I'm going to tell the pilot to star for home."

"Home," Ralston said. He couldn't keep the bitterness from his voice.

"Home," insisted Nels Bernssen. "Not the University. *Home*."

"You'll be there. Leonore will, too. But I've—what did you mean?" The inflection of Bernssen's words meant more than what he'd said.

"Neither Leonore nor I will be returning to Ilium. I don't think Westcott will, either. We've discussed this, the three of us—and the others, too. We're establishing a private research foundation devoted entirely to further study of the chaos weapon, its cause, effect, origins, everything about it."

"And?" prompted Ralston.

"We want you to be a director. In charge of researching the planetoid's origins, the race that built it, things of that nature."

"Where will the funding come from?" asked Ralston.

"We won't have any trouble finding it," said Bernssen. "Putting together what we know about chaos gives us a fantastic spectrum of products to market. Westcott can predict weather, or so he claims, given enough parameters for his equations."

"What about the Nex? We promised them a first look at the information in our research papers."

"I don't know about you, Dr. Ralston, but I don't intend publishing for free anything that might bring us enough money to do as we please for the rest of our lives. We might consider selling the Nex some of our predictions for bargain rates. But papers? Why publish trade secrets? We don't have to publish any longer. Unless we want. I called the shots when I took the money to fund this expedition and didn't guarantee anything to anyone. In fairness, I suppose we'll give the sponsors first grab at some of the things we produce—the predictions— but we don't have to dance to anyone's tune but our own."

"This is so big, Nels."

"I know. And we're lucky to have Leonore in it with us. She has incredible skills she's hidden away." He smiled sheepishly. "She didn't want to frighten me away with her brilliance, I suppose. But she was raised by one of the foremost entrepreneurs on Nova Terra. If she can't handle the business for us, she knows the people who can—and can hire them away from her father. The man's not well liked."

"But this affects so much," said Ralston. "If Westcott can predict weather, we can do sociological dynamics studies to predict wars. Maybe even determine how to stop them."

"There's that," agreed Bernssen. "And more. So much more we'll still be figuring them out a hundred years from now."

"Director of Archaeology?" asked Ralston.

"Or whatever title suits you. Results are what we need at first, to establish credentials and start the money flowing. Then we can funnel a limitless flood of funding into pure research. And we will!"

"Get the pilot started for Novo Terra," said Ralston. "I can't wait to return!"

Nels Bernssen slapped Ralston on the shoulder, then left. The archaeologist settled back in his bunk, mind unable to seize on any single fact and think about just that. So much had happened.

The chaos weapon was destroyed by its own existence, but it had taken with it countless lives. Ralston thought it was only fitting that some good come from the destruction it had wrought.

He smiled at the thought of Salazar's reaction. The man would be livid at losing Nels, Leonore, and especially Westcott, not to mention the others in the expedition. As Francis Bacon had written, "Revenge is a wild kind of justice." At last Ralston would get justice from the school. The University of Ilium's faculty would be banging on their doors, begging for research positions.

The Chaos Foundation? Ralston liked the sound of it.

He pulled taut the restraining straps when the pilot announced the shift. The sensory scrambling that had proven so beneficial in dealing with controlling the chaos field now sent him spinning in dizzying circles, tasting sound and hearing the touch of the bunk against his body. But Michael Ralston didn't care.

A universe lay beyond such momentary confusion, a universe defined by chaos controlled!